MW01113547

aspects of the
NOVEL
a novel

Some Other Books by David R. Slavitt

Fiction

Get Thee to a Nunnery
The Cliff
Turkish Delights
Short Stories Are Not Real Life
Lives of the Saints
Salazar Blinks
Alice at 80
Jo Stern
King of Hearts
Anagrams

Poetry

Falling from Silence
PS3569.L3
Epic and Epigram:
Two Elizabethan Entertainments
A Gift
Crossroads
Eight Longer Poems
Equinox
The Walls of Thebes

Translations

Propertius in Love: The Complete Poetry
The Book of Lamentations
Sonnets of Love and Death by Jean de Sponde
The Book of Twelve Prophets
The Oresteia of Aeschylus
The Hymns of Prudentius
Sixty-One Psalms of David
The Metamorphoses of Ovid
Ovid's Poetry of Exile
The Eclogues and the Georgics of Virgil

Anthologies

The Complete Greek Drama (with Palmer Bovie)
The Complete Roman Drama (with Palmer Bovie)

aspects of the
NOVEL
a novel

by David R. Slavitt

CATBIRD PRESS

First edition

CATBIRD PRESS
16 Windsor Road, North Haven, CT 06473
800-360-2391; catbird@catbirdpress.com
www.catbirdpress.com

Our books are distributed by
Independent Publishers Group

This book is a work of fiction, and the characters and
events in it are fictitious. Any similarity to real persons,
living or dead, is coincidental and not intended by the author.

Library of Congress Cataloging-in-Publication Data

Slavitt, David R., 1935-
Aspects of the novel : a novel / by David R. Slavitt.
p. cm.
ISBN 0-945774-56-7 (hardcover : alk. paper)
1. Middle aged men—Fiction. 2. Funeral rites and
ceremonies—Fiction. 3. Commencement ceremonies—Fiction. 4.
Depression, Mental—Fiction. 5. Fathers and sons—Fiction. 6.
Novelists—Fiction. 7. Weddings—Fiction. I. Title.
PS3569.L3 A87 2003
813'.54—dc21
                              2002006912

But then, of course, life stories, and the avoidance of life stories, were integral to Freud's work, both clinically and theoretically. The life story was, in part, the ways in which a person avoided having a life story. How we escape from our lives is our life, and how our lives tend to resist our stories about them was what interested Freud.

—Adam Phillips, *Darwin's Worm*

I. In the Riff Mountains

1

I'm Mina Hall.

It is perfectly possible that someone else in the auditorium could actually be saying this and even meaning it, but what I meant to express – may be said to have said – was "I'm in a hall." Words are the things between the spaces, but one doesn't put spaces into speech, even interior monologue.

Even that rule is not reliable, however, as we know from the example of The King of France's Hat, in which "The King of France," spaces and all, becomes a single word. (There could of course be a woman named Frances – or a man named Francis – whose bedraggled fedora is the dwelling place of a hypothetically anthropomorphic and megalomaniac flea that, having declared itself to be monarch of all it surveys, is the king of Frances' hat, but never mind.)

Mina Hall, having briefly flickered into life, expires, one of those tiny tadpoles devoured by some passing pickerel or big-mouthed bass within instants of its having emerged from the egg, the whole universe there and then not there. Poof!

That was how it began, but what was "it"? A novel, I am ashamed to say. Ashamed, because which of us believes in novels anymore? All those tedious descriptions of objects — furniture, china, flatware, clothing (including, every now and then, underwear), in order to suggest a verisimilitude that the author will only squander as he or she manipulates the protagonist into a satisfactory denouement so that, somehow, the moral conventions of the genre are satisfied: good characters getting at least an approximate kind of reward, while for the wicked ones there is some manner of comeuppance. And we are too old for such foolishness. Anyway, I am.

Younger, I could at least pretend to belief. Now, I no longer have the energy or the patience. Either wiser or, just as probably, more spiritually sluggish, I find myself wondering idly whether there might be a novel that describes a small, discrete, almost insignificant action, in which, at the crucial moment, the hero decides, say, to wear the blue tie rather than the red.

Who could possibly care?

Ah, but let us suppose a couple of desperado kids are lurking at the corner, Leopold and Loeb types, which is to say that they are philosophical criminals, as full of doubt as I am myself about the connections between cause and effect, or between actions and their consequences. And let us imagine that they have agreed between them that they will set upon the first man they see who has, knowingly or not, identified himself as a frivolous dandy and an enemy of the proletariat, putting on airs and, say, a red tie…?

Silly?

Oh, yes, of course. But suggestive, too, perhaps. (And even, for all we know, true. Where is it written authoritatively that the world is not silly?)

Would such a novel be worth doing?

Probably not, but it would be something to type, something with which to maintain the illusion that one was still a writer. One might, with no great expectations, plod on.

That ability to plod is, I am afraid, the novelist's main gift. (Poets sprint; novelists slog.)

Gift or curse?

In any event, readers are not usually afflicted in this manner.

In a hall I am, watching as the graduates are called, one at a time, for their degrees to be awarded. Formally, with their middle names even, they are summoned to the stage. Seriatim, they stride up and across its considerable width, which takes rather a long time and is becoming tedious. Could they not confer these degrees en bloc? But then, I tell myself (not because I care but because this interior monologue is more diverting than the external ceremony), at these prices the parents deserve an isolated instant of pride in their child's accomplishment. And a photo op. (But what good flashbulbs can do at these distances is beyond imagining.)

My musings are not so deep, however, as to prevent my hearing the provost call out "Steve and Lee O'Grady" and I look up to see – what? A pair of Siamese twins? Have Chang and Eng come back to study law?

Of course not. No such diversion is on offer. It isn't Steve and Lee, but only the one O'Grady. (Only the one Sordello, Robert Browning, and hang it all, Ezra Pound.)

We all scream for ice cream; it's the same triste trope: tmesis, which may sound like a disease but is not dangerous. An eke-name becomes a nickname. Al oud turns into a lute. The consonant migrates from the article to the adjective and we get, in what is not yet Standard English, a whole nother locution, which is tmesis with an infix.

Stephen Lee crosses the stage and, as he has no doubt been coached, extends his left hand to receive the diploma while he shakes hands with the president with his right. (He "makes mit glass pants," as the immigrant said in my father's joke, meaning "clasp hands," and that, too, was an instance of tmesis.)

Lee, as an independent being, is gone, cruelly robbed of his wraith-like existence like Mina or that poor tadpole. Or the Siamese twin they sacrificed at Children's Hospital of Pennsylvania to give the surviving sibling a chance, however remote. She died, too, about a year and a million dollars later. A brutal business, this. (Surgery, I meant, but so, too, are the tricks that words can play.) At the very moment he was to have received his Juris Doctorate, he is undone, unmanned, unmade. Cain and Abel, all over again.

I am angry with the brutal Steven L. O'Grady, and then not so angry, for abruptly he too is gone. He has disappeared or, worse, has fled to the original tohu and bohu of the uncreated, for I catch myself wondering whether I might have dozed off there for a moment and how they might have passed the Gs and already reached the Os, but it isn't Stephen Lee – or Leigh? – O'Grady but his homonymous doppelganger, Steven Leo Grady.

This is a massacre. A bloodbath of Homeric extravagance. The Trojan spear that enters through O'Grady's eye
comes out the back of his head just above the base of the
skull … Disgusting! His bronze armor resounds with a
dismal clangor as he falls into the dust in a heap.

My mind is wandering. My body is captive here, but
the real me – assuming for a moment there may be such a
thing – is elsewhere. I'm Mona Hill, who is, perhaps, Mina
Hall's sister, who later married the mysteriously famous
Sam. (What in the Sam Hill was he famous for?)

But Ida Gress.

I should grow up, or at least sit up and pay attention. An
eminent avocado has dignified the occasion, addressing us
on the burning questions of the day. (That burning of questions was one of the possibilities the Inquisition considered
but rejected as too severe, even for them.) I remind myself
that this is serious business and these are serious people and
serious times, which call for drastic measures. Cooler heads
must prevail! Not mine, clearly. Capital froideur is not my
long suit. I have a long suit, of course, my best worsted,
which is not the contradiction in terms one might expect.
I am wearing it now, in fact and in fiction, too, and it feels
like a disguise. And how the elephant got into Groucho's
pajamas, we'll never know. Or to elevate the discussion, we
can cite Rimbaud who proclaimed *Je est un autre*, which
can be a preference as easily as a complaint. Indeed, I find
it soothing.

On the way here this morning, it struck me that if this
is the end of my son's childhood, it may mark the beginning of my own second childhood. Or the one I never had,
for which of us does? Or if we did, were we not too young

to appreciate it? Or too stupid? (That was perhaps how we endured it.)

As I made my way through the traffic, I noticed how the light kept changing. Not the traffic signals but the light of day, what God created with a word. But the veritas of the lux is by no means straightforward, and there would be a cloud, every now and again, that would palm the sun, which later reappeared like the coin of a conjurer – whom we may specify, if we choose, as that eminent Arab fakir P. Kabou.

My mood was changeable, too, with bright moments of pride (because my son has succeeded and done what my father wanted me to do) alternating with sudden episodes of dismay, for I turn out to have been an irrelevance, an inconvenient delay ... Had my father been able to produce my son without any awkward intercalation on my own part, how much happier all three of us might have been!

What called out to Ulysses with irresistible appeal was his awareness that his ears, body, and brain were the sirens' universe. They could perform only when some sailor happened by. Alone, on their own, they were mute as the gray wet stones upon which they hunkered down, longing for the arrival of that masculine stranger through whom and for whom they might express themselves. Otherwise, they were no more than dreams, the silent figments of their own imaginations.

That, I suspect, was what Ulysses must have found so reassuring, because, until then, even though he would not have fretted about the possibility that he was a figment, he might never have been certain that he mattered to anyone as much as he mattered to himself. Each of us assumes that he is the hero of his own epic. Or novel. We take that for granted. But we accept only reluctantly and with some chagrin the corollary proposition – that we are secondary characters or bit players or merely extras in everyone else's scripts. What was unsettling for me was to realize that I might be a secondary character in my own story.

2

On his travels in the Riff Mountains, I can see Leo staring at one of the billboards for Ulysse Rent-a-Car: You lease; I lease; we all lease … from Ulysse.

Are the signs multilingual? Does the paronomasia translate?

But the more important question that you may deign to ask is, what he is doing in there in those exotic mountain fastnesses.

What else but fleeing for his life and trying to find in those barren heights – like Gauguin, like Rimbaud – some refuge from the malign furies pursuing him so relentlessly.

That this is melodramatic and even childish is okay. It's the way novels start, or at least those that I remember liking so much back when I was young and read in more innocent ways – although even then, as I turned the pages to follow the twists and turns of the story, a part of me knew that it would all come right in the end. The wounds of the world would be bound up by the time I arrived at the volume's binding.

Those novels still start that way, I presume, but my tastes have changed.

Now that my child is grown and gone, however, I can perhaps resume my own childhood and romp again with piles of books like those I used to lug home from the library. I can revive my imaginary playmates. Rejecting my parents (turn-about is fair play), I can conjure up the life their changeling has been leading in the home that ought rightfully to have been my own. Which of us has not entertained such a notion, even going as far as to suppose an alter ego who is longing (stupidly, stupidly!) for the life to which we have been consigned by some silly clerical error in the divine bureaucracy?

I ought to be far away from here, living a better and truer existence in cleaner and purer air ... in the mountains. With one of those staves that the mountaineers carry, decked with bells to warn off the bears that forage in the foothills. Making their way up and down the steep defiles, adventurers, smugglers, and fugitives from the long arm of the law may be suspicious of one another, but still we carry on like gentlemen, true to the code of the great outdoors.

My notion of mountains is vague, I admit, but how complicated can they be? Hills, steep paths, no paths, hard places to get to ... I sprained my ankle once, when I was eight or nine. It was not a serious wound, not life-threatening anyway, but my left foot was in enormous pain. Useless really. I hopped as well as I could on the right foot, but I was six blocks or so from my house, and that's a long way for a little boy to hop, even with rests. Every now and then, I'd need to put my left foot down for balance, and the sheet of pain that wrapped itself like a burning puttee from ankle to knee was unendurable. But also unimpeachable. Real life (at last!). Would I make it home? Would I collapse and sit down, waiting for my parents to notice my absence, begin to worry, send out a search party to find me, the police or, even better, a large dog with a brandy cask at his neck?

That's what the mountains are like, I imagine, but the search parties are probably unfriendly. Will they help you or just rob you and leave you to die? And the fugitives, hiding in caves, are not tweedy gentlemen like Mr. Ransom and Mr. Tate, but desperadoes hoping not to be found. This is what Rimbaud would have discovered, while Verlaine's scouts were beating the bushes everywhere, having been offered unimaginable sums by the older poet to bring that boy's ass back to Paris.

But as I imagine him, he has tied a handkerchief around his head, has been bronzed by the wind and sun, and has learned a smattering of Arabic, enough, at any rate, so he can pass for a somewhat feebleminded native.

He sits in the bar, drinking a coffee and smoking kif. Leo, across the room, near the side door, sips a chipped bowl of tea. They do not know each other, but each is considering the commencement of a conversation. No big thing, nothing like a friendship. They are too cagey for that, too well defended, having been too much abused. What each has in mind is a casual exchange of pleasantries between two Europeans in this African outland.

But the moment passes, and Leo puts a coin on the table and slips out silently by the side door we have conveniently placed there for him.

He has no idea what he has missed – a short and inconsequential conversation with the young Frenchman and then, for years, the opportunity to lecture at universities in the United States about that last, mysterious phase of the young poet's career. He'd have been a great success, because what scholars like most in poets is silence. A writer who keeps on writing is a nuisance, and the academics have to work hard to keep up. They resent having to apply themselves so strenuously to deconstruct his torrent of words. But silence, as John Cage so impishly discovered, is less demanding and into it one can read whatever *profondeur* one likes.

Outside, under pitiless stars, Leo makes his way along the steep path, but the going is not easy. There is scree, a word I don't get to use very often, and, even more dangerous, there are those small declivities from which stones have been dislodged by the smugglers' mules. In one of these he steps the wrong way, spraining his ankle. In great pain, he hops, a few feet at a time, back toward the inn, toward home, resting and then hopping, and from time to time putting the hurt foot down and feeling the sheet of pain that rises up to wrap his calf from ankle to knee ...

The pain is bad; there is something familiar about it, too, a peculiarly endearing rightness.

Oh, brother!

It is an odd locution, that mild oath. But it reminds us that the person who is and is not another self is holy. Monks call themselves brothers, as do Masons, even when not in their jars. There is, between brothers and sisters, a reaching out for sympathy, understanding, loyalty and affirmation, and there is, almost inevitably, a failure. As with Cain and Abel, Ishmael and Isaac, Esau and Jacob, Leah and Rachel, and Joseph and all his brothers, that fraternity of ruffians who sold him into bondage.

And Steve and Leo?

Them two? Them, too.

I do not have a brother. Only a sister, an only sister. To whom I do not speak.

If thine eye offend thee, pluck it out! Or, to be less radical, tooth. And then, in a curious process of adaptation, one learns to love the empty space, exploring with the tongue the interesting emptiness that becomes one's self every bit as much as all those boring incisors, canines, cuspids, and bicuspids that were original issue. Something like that has happened to me with my sister, and perhaps to her with me. Our estrangement has taken on an identity, has become that faithful and understanding sibling each of us hoped for and ought to have been.

She is not here to witness these commencement exercises. Her absence, however, is a comfort for which I suppose I should be grateful.

Leo? Lee? Leigh? Or even, for that matter, Li? Many Oriental students of the history of the United States of America believe General Lee to have been Asian, for nowhere, even in the most capacious texts and biographies, does one find that necessary tidbit of information – Robert E. Lee was not Chinese. Negative knowledge is difficult to come by.

Leo Grady spent some years on a Fulbright Scholarship, studying collective farming in Denmark, an interesting phenomenon about which there had been nothing whatever in "the literature." He wrote a brilliant proposal, which was approved and funded, and he took himself off to Denmark where, in various bars and restaurants, he asked a number of the locals whether they had ever heard of any collective farms anywhere in the country. He might have occasioned a smile or two from those beside him at the opulent smorgasbords to which his generous stipend gave him entree, but no one had heard of any. Because there weren't any. And when the term of his fellowship expired, he wrote this information on a postcard and sent it back to the Fulbright people.

There was some consternation, but the turnover in the staff had been sufficient to blur whatever blame so that it didn't attach to anyone in particular. And negative knowledge is a kind of contribution, too. Polar bears in Kansas? The rain forests of Delaware? These are perfectly legitimate categories of investigation, but only the pure in heart can pursue these studies which are, therefore … like unicorns.

Actually, it was his brother, Steve, who thought of it. But Steve didn't want to waste two years in Denmark living on open-faced sandwiches and guzzling beer. He was, at the time, in love with U Nu's grandniece, Maisie.

What? Maisie knew?

It is never in good taste to make jokes about people's names. Almost certainly, they've heard them before, although in this case, not having read Henry James, she hadn't – or, more likely, had heard it but hadn't got it.

3

Let us suppose that even in these dismal times, there can still be a book written for intelligent people, sympathetic readers without any preconceived ideas about what ought to happen. A book, that is to say, beyond genre, so that it is neither novel, nor essay, nor even – heaven help us – an extended prose poem. Just a book, zero-grade writing that keeps discovering itself, making itself up as it goes along, unpredictable to me and, therefore, to you as well.

Imagining the book is difficult enough; imagining readers for it, even harder.

❖

In an enormous house, after a party, I am wandering about in the kitchen, which is equipped with the kinds of appliances one generally finds in hotels and restaurants. The staff seem to be … indulgent. They let me know that they don't care if I nibble a little from the huge platters of smoked fish and other dainties. They are not positively helpful, and I can't find any plates or flatware, but they seem not to be troubled even if I eat with my hands. The only worry they have that I am at all aware of is that I may try to engage them in conversation about the family that owns the place. I assure them that I am not interested in the intimate details of the household but am just hungry. They disbelieve me but are nevertheless tolerant, or perhaps even cruelly amused by my efforts to pick bits of smoked salmon and whitefish from the heaping plates and feed myself without getting covered with the oily fish.

A dream, but what is this about? I have no way of knowing. Usually, the worst possible interpretation, the most frightening or distressing, is correct. After all, the mind doesn't bother to repress innocuous stuff. Whatever the psyche buries may be presumed to be unpleasant, if not actually toxic.

Obviously, I am an outsider here, an intruder or an impostor, for otherwise I'd be out with the guests or the members of the family. I am not even certain that my protestations about indifference to the intimate details of the household are sincere. Am I a reporter? A spy of some kind? Am I looking for nourishing tidbits and, in the effort to acquire them, fouling myself with the oils of the smoked fish?

Something like that, no doubt. We sunder, fly apart, fragment from unified individuals into unruly and chaotic constituencies. Ego, Superego, and Id, or call them, as easily and as accurately, Larry, Moe, and Shemp. Harpo, Chico, and Groucho.

Or are there only the two, the self and the other? Laurel and Hardy. Abbott and Costello. Or our very own Steve and Leo. How many of us have a sibling from whom we are separated, to whom we no longer speak? By their very existence, these alter egos indict us if only because they did not make the mistakes we made, have not committed our crimes, and are not responsible for our failures. Which is why the sight of one's doppelganger is always dismaying.

Look, this is my nose, and that is his nose, a perfect replica of mine. It is never with delight that we make such an observation, but in guilt and fear. Yearning, perhaps, too, but it is a hopeless yearning. Steve cries out, O *Leo, Leo, Leo.*

Apparently, Steve has had to learn to yodel in these mountains. The only alternative would have been lugging about those enormous horns with which the natives signal to each other to warn of avalanches or send out for more cough drops. At night, you can hear the strange sounds that echo back and forth in the dry riverbeds, Wadi Ya-noh, Wadi Ya-sei, and Wadi Yagonidu.

❖

Dreams are supposed to give way, though, to a reasonable daytime reality. Mine don't. Instead, I find myself walking through a different kind of nightmare, booby-trapped, mined. (The booby-trapped mind?) There are snipers on the roofs of nearby buildings. (Surprisingly good, that

Manlicher-Carcano, but then that's why Lee chose it.) I go out on the most innocuous errand, and any little thing can set them off, these attackers who think of themselves, of course, as defenders, partisans, loyalists, heroes! It is like living in downtown Priština, where going out to get a fresh bottle of water is a life-or-death gamble. Stefan and Leo are of course on different sides, as is only too common in a civil war.

Salmon mousse is what they are fighting about, really. There are other issues, the religious and political and ethnic and linguistic divisions between the Bosnians, the Serbs, the Croats, the Bosnian Serbs, the Croatian Bosnians, the Serbotian Bosñeros, the ethnic Albanians, and all the other carefree Kosovars ... But the basic quarrel was over a salmon mousse that Stefan's wife, Blooma, had made for her guests. And Leo was visiting at the time with his wife, Lumpka, and – wouldn't you know – after they arrived, hungry, thirsty, and tired, having come all the way from Garage-Door, they saw in the refrigerator that nice salmon mousse molded in the shape of a salmon.

"Perhaps we shouldn't touch it," Lumpka wondered.

"Ach, but would my own brother deny me foodt? [The accent in which I hear this is probably specious, but the last word comes out somewhere between 'food" and "foot," and I like it that way.] His house is my house! My house is his house. His foot is my foot."

He is passionate but nonetheless ridiculous, and it is difficult not to smile as we translate his words back to what he means.

"Eat, eat," Leo insists. "Stefan would be deeply hurt to think we had even hesitated."

So saying, he scoops a handful of fish off the platter and shoves it into his mouth. Whatever she might have thought before, Lumpka is now faced with a quite different situation. The mousse, no longer pristine, looks very good, she is very hungry, and there is now less reason not to allow herself at least a little taste ...

But Blooma and Stefan had been saving that mousse for the visit of the Voivod and his wife, who have promised to drop by for a few minutes before they go together to the annual dinner in memory of the heroic resistance the town had managed for eight days against the invasion of the Visigoths in the eleventh century. (On the ninth day, the Visigoths breached the walls, set fire to the women, raped the horses, and killed the buildings: this was still the early days of the campaign and they were not yet expert in these punitive techniques.)

But the mousse is ruined. Handfuls of it have been scooped out by those pigs! Leo the louse and Lumpka ... the lump! Blooma scoops what is left of the mousse into a bowl, sets the bowl onto a platter, spreads some crackers around the rim, and brings it in to serve. But later on, she and Stefan give the brother and sister-in-law a piece of her mind, hurling at them the truly eloquent Bosnian curses, which have a mannerist vividness that cannot be translated into other languages. Leo and Lumpka leave, storming out of the house. In a huff. A snit. High dudgeon. In a trice! And for good.

When the war comes, it is only an excuse, a flimsy pretext for doing what everyone else is doing anyway. They drop into their local Army and Navy store and pick up a poncho, a canteen, a collection of impressive campaign hats, a few gaudy insignia to sport on their epaulettes and merit-badge sashes, and a clutch of Kalashnikovs. Also a few cases of surplus American Claymore mines (thoughtfully labeled: "This Side Toward Enemy"). Now they can continue the family discussion in more sincere and candid terms. The causus belly (as it were) seems in retrospect all the more plausible, for after the first few months of the siege, who in Kosovo would not have killed for a handful of salmon mousse?

The populace were squabbling amongst themselves for the emaciated corpses of the animals in their zoo cages. There was an epidemic of jokes about cannibalism, as if their repetition might eventually remove some of the opprobrium that generally attaches to the exploitation of this all too available protein resource.

And on the way to the store for a bottle of dog milk or a tin of pickled goat lips, one heard the chatter of repeating rifles perseverating their Senecan vision of the indifference of the gods and the limitlessness of the horrors mankind can contrive to inflict upon itself.

No, there was no war. My sister and I had no such excuse. Or opportunity. But there was a salmon mousse.

Perhaps that was the fish soiling my hands in the dream? I can understand, at any rate, the reticence of those servants about the family that employed them.

4

These commencement exercises are boring enough to allow me to suppose that in each brainpan in the hall there may be an alternate version of my miasmic universe, an interesting and unique series of low-level ravings or high-pitched keenings as the neurons fire, discharging whatever ammunition they have managed to store up. It's a psychic intifada. Living off the land, they are like their colleagues, those fat cells that store up energy, but these hoard ideas and emotions with which, at such moments of intellectual dearth or emotional stress, the organism may continue for a while not only to sustain itself but also to fight back. Those who suffer from Tourette's syndrome bear a slightly heavier burden than the rest of us, but what happens to them happens to us, too. Into every head there comes, willy-nilly, a series of monsters and demons to celebrate ancient victories, mourn old defeats, carry on their guerrilla campaign of buffoonery and *babouinisme*, and, in rowdy reunion, relive old bloody campaigns.

Willie Nilly? Sure, I remember him. Old Bill Nilly, lazy and silly ... What do you suppose ever became of him?

Not that I ever knew such a fellow, but I split apart, becoming both performer and audience as I try to pass the time by telling myself stories I have never heard before, or by making up stories that will somehow surprise even so tough and experienced an audience as myself. Inasmuch as the performer can seldom surpass a certain minimal level of competence, the audience must also perform, pretending to be just a little stupider than the fellow up on stage as the two of them joke back and forth about the awkwardness of their relationship. The one in the spotlight indulges himself in old-fashioned stage maneuvers, tapping the microphone and asking, "Is this on?" Or he resorts to stagy asides, announcing in an eloquent hiss: "But soft now! Someone is coming ... "

Monsieur Neely! Enchanté de vous voir!

M. Neely presents – why not? – a wine list and goes immediately into his impressive spiel, rambling on about old and new wood of fine or coarse grain and of light, medium, or dark toast, and explaining how long the grapes have macerated and whether or not they were picked before or after the rain, which is, of course, important.

Mona inquires about a Côtes de Nuits, and giggles.

Guillaume is not flustered – he never is – and answers her with poise and charm, without correcting her about her confusion, *Côtes* meaning something quite different from *manteaux* or *robes*. She doesn't care, having imagined an article of apparel, a gay negligee, let us say, that has wandered, no doubt through someone's negligence, from the bedroom to make its surprising appearance here below in the *salle à manger*.

Beside her, Leo contrives to hide his distaste for her stupid joke. He looks up in exasperation and notices that there is an enormous hole in the roof. The restaurant is evidently one of those theme-park experiences, and the pretense here is that the food is being served in a huge derelict building, perhaps in the tropics. In the sky above their table, large dentate leaves are looming. The size of the plants is positively fearsome, and the effect is, to say the least, dramatic. Inside the building's shell, there are electrical cables hanging from the broken beams of what remains of the ceiling.

In as calm a manner as he can manage, Leo suggests to Mona, "We seem to be inhabiting someone else's dream."

Although he is perfectly serious, she only giggles.

Bill, whose dream this actually is, brings out the wine, opens the bottle, presents Leo with the cork, pours a slosh into Leo's glass, and waits for the patron's approval: the correct quick sip and cursory nod. The point now isn't for Leo to decide whether he approves of his own choice, sloshing the liquid in the goblet, sniffing its nose, and rolling his first sip around the various precincts of his tongue, but only whether the wine he has chosen has gone off or not. If it's vinegar, Bill will take it back. But if the wine is acceptably what it was supposed to be, then he will pour it down the retching throat of the ignorant patron who knows nothing about wine or good manners or, indeed, anything else. Who needs to be taught a lesson. Who, having lost all rights, has become, suddenly, an occasion for the staff's pranks and a source of diversion and instructive entertainment for the other patrons.

These draconian measures are required because the whole notion of the restaurant is predicated upon tactlessness. What decent people, after all, would come to an expensive establishment that called itself Sarajevo and offered the sounds of small arms fire and occasional heavy artillery rounds instead of the usual Muzak, providing as well such special effects as the flickering lights and the mismatched china and flatware? What Sarajevo promises and delivers is the fun of the end of the world without the actual danger. How better to enjoy a meal than to be, as the eastern mystics say, wholly in the moment? And how on earth to do that except in a war zone, where each meal, which may well be one's last, is a special treat, all the more delicious because of the suffering and rage that surround the dining room's precarious island of calme, luxe, and volupté?

They were going to call it The War Zone, but attorneys representing a rough-trade bar across town threatened legal action, so that Bill and his partners came up with Sarajevo instead. The busboys limp a bit and wear head bandages. The candles on the tables provide, now and again, the only illumination in the dining room. Most of the items on the menu are fictitious, or so many of the diners hope.

Few of them order the salmi de rat, the terrine de chien, or the blanquette de faux vaux (whatever that is). Off the menu, the waitress explains sotto voce, there are other offerings, less adventurous, less unconventional, including, *par exemple*, the vrai vaux, the beef, the lobster, the lamb, and the fresh whole fish, boned at the table. She is able to provide these rare delicacies to particularly important and valuable customers. Doris – her name is on a pin on her lapel – explains that the cook will give her almost anything in exchange for a few minutes of her time now and then in the pantry (boned at the table!) or against the wall of the vegetable refrigerator. She sighs wearily, letting them know that it's no fun for her, just part of the job. She does what she has to do.

Mona is not giggling anymore. This is … in bad taste!

Of course it is, which is why business has been so good. As Leo discovered, reservations are not easy to get.

"He's a hunchback," Doris confides in Leo, with a suggestive wink. (But what is she suggesting? Is she implying that this makes it more disagreeable? Or more fun? Or lucky? Does she suppose that it is Leo who has a thing for hunchbacks? He tries in any event to look sympathetic.)

There is a wail of not so distant sirens but this, too, turns out merely to be part of the décor. Doris, pad in hand, is ready for their orders.

5

Lift. Glide. Narrative impetus. How, except by tired and distasteful artifice, can I achieve this? The appeal to the reader's interest in plot may be vulgar, but it is reliable. The unsophisticated are not contemptible, and there are some of us who, while we are not like them, can still, for all our refinement, feel a nostalgia for narrative with its vicissitudes and surprises. What happens next? Or, more particularly, what happens next to these characters in whom we have invested, however tentatively and conditionally, our feelings? And if one thing happens and then another happens afterwards, what connects the two events?

"The king died, and then the queen died of grief," is the textbook example, but how do we know for sure that it was grief that did her in or even tipped the scale, bringing her shadowy existence to its premature conclusion?

It may be what the writer believes or even what we should like to believe, ourselves, but, if the truth be told, we cannot even say with certainty how or even whether cause and effect operate in the world in which we have lived for so long: in moments of stress we admit, to ourselves if to no one else, our ignorance and all but utter helplessness. No one believed Cassandra, even though she was always right, because no one would concede that it was all there for her to see, predestined and foreordained.

The question of belief is, quite literally, vital. Without some faith in what one is doing and experiencing, there is no life. The air one breathes is as useless as it would be to a fish. The soul fails, and the body deteriorates. The queen doesn't just miss the king but misses herself, cannot recognize her own face in the mirror. Her food and drink are tasteless and do not nourish. The rooms of the palace are strange to her, installations by some museum curator whose tastes she cannot share. Objects once dear to her have turned suddenly to expensive junk, as if all the authentic pieces had been taken and replicas had been supplied, identical in every respect except that they were somehow diminished in value precisely because they were copies.

It pains me to think of my son, whose commencement I am here to observe, as he was a few years ago – off in a warehouse in North Dakota having just such a crisis of spirit, far away, beyond all help or succor, going up and down the aisles of that enormous entrepôt with his clipboard in hand, looking impressive but feeling himself to be an impostor. I afflict myself deliberately, imagining it, as if the discomfort I feel could change anything, could do him any good at all. I'd have given anything to know of his distress, even if I could not actually have done anything to protect him or to diminish his pain. I could have offered my encouragement, sympathy, and love, none of which could have been of any practical value but might have been welcome, nevertheless.

There he is, in this Antonioniesque dreamscape, pallets piled high with cartons of canned goods and great sacks of grain, and men in blue jumpers and hardhats scurrying up and down the aisles with their hydraulic dollies and bright yellow forklifts, and he is taking notes.

It is his first job out of college, and I give him credit – and take some, too, as any parent would – for he has learned quickly enough that in what we call the "real world," there is a great deal of imposture. He is pretending to be a management consultant. The firm for which he works is pretending to consult, with young men in suits, carrying briefcases and clipboards, making observations, and taking

what appear to be scientific and mathematical measurements of efficiency. The underlying truth of the situation
is nonetheless apparent to all parties, who, if only for the
etiquette of it, agree to the pretense, even though they
understand that nobody calls in a consulting firm when the
operation is profitable. So they're losing money. And the
solution is to increase revenues (which they've already
thought of) or to cut costs. They've thought of that, too,
but cutting costs is unpleasant because it means firing
people, and it is convenient to have a firm of outsiders upon
whom management can put the blame.

So, the result of all these time-and-motion studies is
foreordained. It does not take a Cassandra to see that there
will be a recommendation that the work force be cut by a
third. And that will have the effect of scaring the hell out
of the remaining two thirds, who will work harder and, even
with their numbers reduced, still get the job done, whatever it is. But the consulting firm can't just tell people this.
They have to look as though this is a conclusion they
arrived at by dint of objective study and analysis. So they
hire a gang of kids, impose a stringent dress code on them,
and send them off to look studious and analytic. They're
putting on a show, out there in Fargo, at the Pro-Vendor
company (they must also have hired an outfit, one supposes,
in order to come up with that snappy name for themselves).

But there he is, in his suit and tie (two more ties back
in the motel room, and the other suit, and however many
shirts it will take to get to Friday), with his clipboard and
maybe even a stopwatch on a lanyard of some kind, and
he's filling out forms and looking at these grown men who
see what he's doing and realize what's coming down, and
hate him, and he can feel their hatred, which he's smart
enough not to take personally, but it still can't feel like

anything other than what it is. He's a threat to their livelihood, to their wives and children, to their crummy flats in Fargo or cabins out on the prairie ...

And he decides that this is not what he is, that he doesn't recognize this as his life, that the face in the motel bathroom mirror only happens to resemble his, and the young man on the warehouse floor looks like him only coincidentally, but this isn't how he sees himself, this isn't what he can live with, and he has to do something about it. And for his making that decision – or, no, not even for making it but for recognizing it and acknowledging its necessity – I am proud of him. Brains and talent are handy but useless without a certain minimal self-respect, and he has that. This boring ceremony here in the law school auditorium is all well and good, but it's almost beside the point, because what we're celebrating, what I'm celebrating anyway, is his refusal that day in Fargo to continue in the cruel imposture in which, up until then, he'd been playing a part.

I'm proud of him, but envious, too, because he's still young enough to be able to change. There comes a time, later, when there can be such moments of revelation but without any opportunity to make the obvious and necessary adaptations.

Or to put it more bluntly, one discovers that one is old.

After that admirable moment of decision, he did something else that worried me at the time but which, in time, I came to understand and even endorse. He began applying to law schools, which was reasonable enough. But he also decided to quit the management consultants' charade, because this was his last opportunity for some years, and maybe even forever, to exploit the few months of freedom that this change in his plans had dropped in his lap. He would go out to Lake Tahoe, get a job selling ski lift tickets, and enjoy the mountains, the scenery, and the free skiing that was one of the fringe benefits of employment out there. He would become, at least for a short while, a ski bum.

It's not something I'd have done. Or could even have imagined. And while I didn't actually disapprove of it, I found it ever so slightly troublesome precisely because of that otherness. Children are not clones, of course, and they come into the world, as any parent discovers, with their own personalities and inclinations. They have their own selfhoods, perhaps, their own destinies, as Cassandra might maintain …

Parents don't object to that, or resent it, but on occasion we become aware of the gulf, that awful separation even from those who are our own flesh and blood. Our chromosomes and genes, their mother's mother's mother's mitochondria, and they might as well have come from some other planet to take up residence in the nursery and astonish us with their unpredictable strangeness.

Some time after Mal's months out there, I was at Lake Tahoe at a conference in which I was only tangentially interested. My real reason for participating had been to see the place, to smell the air, to look at the trees and the flowers, and to watch the marmots scampering across the ground, all of which were unfamiliar to me and had been, at least at first, novelties to my son, as well. The season was different – I was there in the summertime – but the thinness of the air would have been the same, I suppose. Six thousand feet up, one needs to acclimate, to retrain one's heart and lungs, which are unaccustomed to such deprivation. The occasional giddiness, and the more persistent feeling of being on the verge of a headache, were what he'd lived through. In pursuit of fun. (But where is it written that such a goal is in any way dishonorable?)

I, of course, was pursuing him, imagining that by experiencing his discomfort, and that sense of strangeness, I could somehow intuit what might have been going on with him at that crucial moment in his life. But that not quite sick feeling of shortness of breath and dry mouth suggested to me a whole range of human limitations, not just physical but emotional and moral, too. And the mountains are overbearing and out of what we in the east think of as human scale. Cliffs that westerners are proud of and claim for their own, we find intimidating and humbling. Those precipices down near Emerald Bay and Eagle Falls are sights that tourists come to admire, and he would almost certainly have gone to see them. And felt … delight? Awe? Oppression?

We cannot know the interiority of another's experience, even if we exert ourselves, even if we attempt to undergo something similar. The similarity is suggestive, but more likely than not merely misleading.

Younger than I am – children always are – and in better shape, he would have adjusted within a few days, would have looked at the mountains with an altogether different eye, as invitations or as challenges to his skiing abilities. He would have done better out there than I did. He might even have had a good time, speeding down through the silent glare of the steep mountainsides and feeling the rush of the wind that was an external equivalent to the internal exhilaration of the experience of speed and concentrated attention.

Let him go, I tell myself. Let him go and take what delight you can in the possibility that, at least at moments, he was happy out there.

I try to do that. But if it is difficult to imagine another's pain, what is even more challenging a feat is to experience another's happiness. Is that always true? Or is it merely an artifact of my own depression, which wasn't affecting him when he was out there. In any event, what keeps coming back to me – because I am a parent and parents always want it to be better for a child, to be perfect, even – is that the last week he was out there, some son of a bitch stole his expensive ski boots.

What his study of the law has done for him, I have only the vaguest guess. What it has done to him is more accessible, however, for it has given him the tools for the analysis of certain aspects of the human condition, in fact it has all but enforced a particular kind of analysis. It has made him a grown-up in a way I can never be. And have never wanted to be. Those ski boots, for instance, become a piece of personalty with a monetary value that can be determined. One may or may not be able to recoup. Even if he knew who had taken them, he couldn't help figuring out how much the effort would cost to get back that amount of money, or even, by a writ of replevin, the boots themselves. And without even having to break out the calculator, he'd write them off. What he wouldn't do is mourn for the loss of mere objects, albeit objects that had become a souvenir of themselves, vessels of significance because he had been wearing them on the mountain on some splendid run that ended an all but perfect afternoon, and that he alone remembers.

One cannot put a quantifiable value on that. But one can plausibly assert that there is, nonetheless, a value. Indeed, one can say that "value" is simply another word for "love," in which case any quantification, or any other kind of abstraction, is a betrayal.

"I put it to you, sir, that your entire testimony is a tissue of lies!" And as one delivers that delicious line, the sibilance of the antepenultimate word ought to be as menacing as an asp's hiss.

A titter runs through the crowd, which is not actually to say that a small boy makes his way among the spectators, pinching nipples and leering.

"Ordure! Ordure!" Lord Lovaduck calls from the bench, banging his gavel, at the same time calling for quiet and decorum and also expressing his view of the case. He instructs the jury to disregard the entirety of the witness's testimony, which is, of course, impossible. One cannot unring the bell. He might as well have instructed them not to think of Belgium, which is good policy but bad law. "Sir Reginald, pray continue," he says, making only a pro forma attempt to conceal a yawn.

Sir Reginald Fitz-Hyphen adjusts his monocle and says, in a bored drawl, in impossibly refined nasal timbres, "Returning to the question of the salmon mousse ..."

Cut to: Blooma, staring at him in cold fury.

Sir Reginald (VO): " ... that you claim to have been saving for those whom you considered to be more important than members of your own family who were also, I venture to remind you, your guests. On what reasonable basis that you can explain to the ladies and gentlemen of the jury did you make these distinctions? And, in the light of what has happened, would you make the same astonishing and deplorable decision today as you did back then?"

Blooma narrows her eyes in defiance and hatred. "Yes," she says. "Just the same!"

The spectators gasp. Sir Reginald allows the monocle to fall from his eye in a gesture of derision, which we may be allowed to suspect he has practiced. Above him, on the bench, Lord Lovaduck bangs his gavel slowly and all the more menacingly.

"You may call your next witness," he says with a pointed lack of enthusiasm.

6

"John Gorki." He is not a witness, only a graduate. But the name is interesting enough to recall me, at least for the moment, to these interminable proceedings. I look at the young man crossing the stage. A relative, perhaps, of Maxim's? A member of a family that admired the Russian writer and took his name? Or are there many families named Gorki, so that the eminence of the novelist has become an annoyance to other Gorkis, many of whom are not fans.

But why "John" rather than "Ivan" – although, of course, one could as easily ask, why not? The elements combine with the casual assurance of a French sailor's shirt above a pair of blue jeans. Maybe it wasn't the surname that was troublesome to the family, but the tiresome first names. We all know of Maxim Gorki, but few of us have heard of his siblings:

> Aphorism Gorki.
> Epigram Gorki.
> Adage Gorki.
> Apothegm Gorki.
> Proverb Gorki.
> Truism Gorki.
> And the coyly playful sister, Paronomasia Gorki?

And of course, there was Maxim's nemesis, the black sheep of the family, the dorky Gorki, if you will, Cliché Gorki, who never wrote a line but whose words, nonetheless, are always and everywhere on people's lips. But there's always the rotten apple that doesn't fall far from the tree and that you can't compare to an orange, but will spoil the barrel.

Ahem.

Ah, him.

Where was I? Where am I?

Still here, I am afraid, pretending to have assented to this spate of language that goes on almost all the time. If I tell myself that I have invited it or at least permitted it, then I do not have to suppose that I am crazy. This is only a diversion, not an obsession. There is a world of difference between "Je m'amuse," and "Je m'abuse," but only a single letter to distinguish between them.

I can remember thinking that this stream of babble was a gift, was an expression of my most valuable and intimate self. Years, decades later, I am less enthusiastic and have begun to feel a certain envy for those whose minds are comparatively blank, who can sit and wait for a bus or a train with the patience of a turnip, the impassivity of a rock, floating through time with the ease and the grace of dumb beasts. Isn't that the implied promise of landscape painting, that if only we could learn to look, could contrive to invest ourselves wholly into a scene the artist has chosen for us, we could partake at least to some degree in the gorgeous imperturbability of that water, those trees, that stone wall and the elaborately textured surface of the weathered barn in the foreground off to the left. Paintings are, by their nature, quiet.

Or they used to be. Now there are the audio-guides that yammer into the ears of the museums' visitors. An abomination.

Anna Bomination?

No, no. Go away.

And she does, hustled off by two uniformed thugs, Beck and Call, who wait upon me for my beckon call for just such occasions.

She will not be heard from again although, now that she's gone, I begin to miss her a little. She was rather too passive, too complicit in her own undoing, but I admire her refusal to plead with me to keep her around for a page or two.

"I love the dead," was what I thought I heard the announcer on Harvard's FM station say last night as she gave the name of the selection they'd just aired. "By Sir Gay Rachmaninoff." Not too much different from the composer's straight brother, who wrote "Isle of the Dead" using the same notes in the same order. But those spaces between the words you speak can be vertiginous crevasses into which your sled can drop, with all those yapping dogs, and you're whited out in that featureless landscape, gone without a trace, as absolutely absent as Anna.

Nina must suspect but she cannot prove my discomfort and perhaps doubts that I am miserable, if only because it is what she so much wants for me. It would please her immeasurably, which is why I am struggling to keep it to myself. My ex-wife and I see each other only at these ceremonial occasions, which, of course, our meetings poison. Graduations, births, and, in the not too distant future, bar mitzvahs and weddings, the *rites de passage* other people look forward to, are, for us, impending horrors.

One thing I can do is imagine that I am not here but at home, at the word processor, writing this scene, where I would be in control of – not only of myself but of the world around me. Of her, even. I can, by touching a few keys, give her a hot flash or a heart attack, or I can possess her as if I were the devil, and cause her to howl like that banshee I have, on occasion, heard.

What broke us up? I have long ago given up speculating about that. Too many causes or not enough. Or none. We have the vain idea that we live our lives, but it is also true that our lives live us. And we do what we are required to do by that outline near the coaster on the desk where our author is typing away. We may make our suggestions, of course, but who knows what the scenario has in store for us? It is, as I imagine it, an unimpressive scrap of paper with telephone numbers scribbled in the margin and odd notes, some of which are underlined, even though they are all but illegible, even to a Cassandra.

Nina handles herself better than I do. Her posture has been one of more or less righteous indignation, which she has maintained over the years so that, justifiable or not, it has become her habit and seems altogether natural. My predilections are introspective, so that I could always find at least a pretext for feelings of guilt. Of course, I have no way of knowing what she feels. I can only draw inferences from behavior, which I didn't do very well when we were married. For all I know, she may feel guilty, too, but is better at concealing her emotions. For all I know, I may be more successful than I suppose in hiding my feelings. That suave and imperturbable façade I try to maintain may be, at least for the short periods we spend together, persuasive.

That it cannot persuade me doesn't signify, for that was never its purpose. It would be crazy for me to believe my own propaganda.

Ah, but there, you see, my hunch is that she believes hers, and I admire her for it, even envy her for constructing fictions she can inhabit. How many novelists can do that?

Well, Hemingway tried, and Fitzgerald. But as each of them discovered in his own disastrous way, it isn't a good idea.

❖

"You think they'd have known better," Leo says. "You'd think, with that success, they would have had confidence."

"They had it, yes," Stefan says. "They had confidence, youth, and a job. They had everything."

They are standing there in their waiters' uniforms in The Clean Well-Lighted Place, the café where they work and where the old man is drinking his last brandy. It is late, and they are waiting for him to finish so they can go home. This is the old man who tried to commit suicide, tried to hang himself, but his niece cut him down. And he comes to drink here every night and sits at the same table in this famous story.

This is the old man whom Hemingway describes as being deaf, but he says that the man likes the quiet here in the café and tells us, with odd, exquisite delicacy, that he can feel the difference. Even though he is deaf, the quality of the silence here is somehow palpable to him.

It is a brave sentence to put in the first paragraph of a story. And for that sentence one can forgive its author a lot of his foolishness.

"He was in despair," Leo says, explaining the suicide attempt.

"What about?" Stefan says.

"Nothing."

"How do you know it was nothing?"

"He has plenty of money."

And suddenly, in less than half a page, we know an enormous amount about the two waiters and about the old man.

What Stefan and Leo are doing at that altitude, nobody could ever figure out.

But they can understand the older waiter's insomnia, which is his credential of initiation, even his badge of honor.

And if they are puzzled about it, or curious about the despair of which it is a symptom, or those little assaults that life presents to torment those of us who are in despair, they can ask me. I can tell them whatever they want to know. I was up much of the night, lying there in the motel room, listening to the music and the painful pronunciations of the announcers on the Harvard FM station, and dreading today.

7

What I'm doing, I'm afraid, is skittering off, venturing closer by a step or two and then, in fear, backing away. Fear and chagrin. It isn't Nina whom I am unwilling to confront, but Malcolm, my son, whom I ought to have protected, even from myself. I remember thinking, during that sordid business of the divorce, that what was at fault in this "no-fault" process was our freedom and prosperity. In the old country – whatever old country you care to name – nobody got divorced. You had your plot of land, and your mule, and your wife, and you were bound to them all and had no choices. If you weren't happy, too bad. Because there was nothing you could do to change any of these things, you learned somehow to live with them.

Here, now, unhappiness is a crime against nature, a violation of the constitutional obligation – because a right has a nasty way of turning into a duty – to the pursuit of happiness. It is un-American not to be utterly euphoric. And those we would have given our lives to protect are hurt, not in a simple dramatic catastrophe but subtly, insidiously, as their faith in the goodness of the world is broken.

I remember clutching at some intellectual straw an ill wind blew by me – the idea that children of divorce are warier, and that this can provide them with certain adaptive advantages over those who have never been forced to learn the hard lessons that the ruin of a family can teach. I liked hearing that and, even though I knew it wasn't true, enjoyed telling myself that the kids were, in some ways, better off.

And then, a week or two later, I heard from Nina that she had heard from Malcolm's expensive, permissive, cuddling, coddling little school that he was cutting classes, that he was hiding underneath the buildings in the dark of the crawl spaces.

He was … ten? Eleven?

In there, somewhere. And, evidently, not so much better off after all.

❖

For a moment, I nod off.

A Russian, he sounds like – Igor Vasillyev Nodoff, minor acmeist poet of the last days of the last Tsar, who was brutally ignored by the Soviets. (They were, for once, correct in their estimate that Nodoff could do them neither good nor harm.) He went into a deep depression and was unable to write a word for the rest of his life. After his death, however, he was declared to have been a hero of the Russian people, a man whose silence was golden and an act of conscience almost without precedent in literary annals.

The Russians are selling nuclear materials to the Iranians. They are systematically destroying Chechnya. You can read about it in Tolstoy's *Tales of Army Life* and then, later, in *Hadji Murad*, his posthumous novel about the Chechin fight for liberty that is silly enough to make Nodoff's silence an act of aesthetic as much as moral excellence. If only Tolstoy had known when to quit. Or Wordsworth. Or … [fill in the blank].

We suppose, now that the Evil Empire has collapsed, that we are safer, but desperate men will behave as badly as the merely wicked. And less predictably. If you think of the Chechins as Russia's Croats, you can imagine a deterioration that could reduce us all to Nodoff's noble silence.

What is being written about the Jugs is not particularly useful. I saw a recent book, a Rand Study edited by F. Stephen Larrabee, entitled *The Volatile Powder Keg: Balkan Security After the Cold War.*

Mr. Larrabee? (Steve? Frank? Fitzhugh? Fabrizio? Fastolf? It doesn't matter, he seems to be asleep.) What I wanted to ask him was what other kind of powder keg we have to worry about? Isn't it in the nature of powder kegs to be volatile, just as it is the nature of Yugoslavs to kill one another?

I am a good boy. I read this stuff trying to keep myself informed. I want to be a responsible citizen, a grown-up, but it is impossible. They keep setting me off on unpredictable flights. I read that Henry Wijnaendts, the Dutch ambassador to France, was appointed by the E.C. as its special envoy to Yugoslavia, and that his book *Joegoslavische Kroniek* "should be read by any student of the Balkan crisis."

A good idea. Let's all stop. Take a deep breath. And turn our skittish attention to the study of the Dutch language. We can resume our deliberations on the problems of Yugos in two or three years.

Nodoff wasn't heroically silent. He was busy, as likely as not, learning Dutch. Or Finnish. Or calculus. He just got sidetracked somehow. It happens. We get distracted.

As far as that goes, I can imagine that Mynheer Wijnaendts' entire interest in the Joegoslavische problem was a distraction. Why else would a stolid Dutchman occupy himself with the sordid Serbotians and brutal Bosñeros except for the cold comfort he could take from the fact that, whatever the disarray he found in his own domestic life, it paled in comparison with what was going on down there in the Balkans. Was his marriage collapsing? Was his ten-year-old son hiding underneath one of the school buildings? He could look to the catastrophes of the Kosovars, their rapes and murders, their concentration camps and their mass graves, and figure that, at least compared with them, he was not such a bad guy.

It is also possible to take it the opposite way, figure the Kosovars as exemplars of the normal human condition, the savage characteristics of which are in all of us only waiting for their occasion, which has not yet arisen in lives that, so far, have been lucky. It is not at all to our credit that we have behaved better. The vicissitudes of our lives have been such as to allow us to invent all manner of pleasant fictions about nobility and piety and loyalty, which have never been tested. We live, most of us, in a fool's paradise, an unreliable interlude of peace and plenty that has demanded nothing of us in the way of decency or generosity or honor.

The speaker at these commencement exercises went on at some length about the rule of law.

Or was it the rule of thumb – I've got you under my thumb, and you will do what I say, because I make the rules.

A term, the speaker admitted, less of description than of aspiration, which sounds as though he was trying to talk while inhaling.

The Rue l'Oeuflau? It could be an address in Paris or, more likely, in some squalid *quartier* of Algiers where Leo sits and reads in *La Chute*, his favorite journal, an account of how Zairian soldiers in Goma had been shaking down a civilian who refused to pay the modest bribe they had demanded. A group of civilians, thinking it a lapse of taste for this to be done in broad daylight, set upon the two soldiers, beat them to death, tied one of their bodies to the back bumper of a car, and then dragged it to the city.

During the melee, a vehicle owned by World Vision, and three more that belonged to Doctors Without Borders, were hijacked by the unruly crowd. The United Nations, ever alert, has suggested that foreign aid workers take security precautions.

What can those foreign aid workers possibly do? Relocate the whole program to Iceland?

Meanwhile, Haiti could administer the UN operations in Kosovo. They have more experience with barbarity than the Dutch, for instance. (Mr. Wijnaendts' book could not have caused much of a stir among the Haitians.) The first item on their agenda might be the changing of the name of the Kosovars' capital city from the coy irony of Priština to the simpler and more familiar truth of Port Au Let.

How would this be of any help in Goma? It wouldn't. Zaire is beyond help. The rule of law turns out to be a pleasant fiction. In Africa, and throughout the world, the only law you can rely on is that of gravity.

Or maybe fictions are never, by their nature, pleasant. Novels tend to turn out in satisfactory ways, which means that their readers come to expect that all will be well in the end, not only in the pages of the books they hold in their hands but also in the lives they are leading. There is in novels an unwarranted optimism that is not helpful, that affects our judgment by distorting our expectations and encouraging us to take foolish chances. Then, when the happy resolution fails to materialize, we are left to our own devices of self-reproach and chagrin – for if success is the general rule, then it is only failure, the exception, that we can claim as truly our own. The habit of reading novels prompts us toward a belief in progress that was as difficult for those nineteenth-century writers to resist in their time as it is for us to entertain today. Each happy ending we encounter, inviting us to share those antiquated fantasies, puts us at a slightly greater risk of disappointment. We are, after each passage through Dickens or Trollope or Eliot, just a little stupider than we were before, a little less well prepared to cope with the randomness of life's punishments and rewards.

The underlying assumptions of novels may amount to what our speaker would call an "aspiration," but it's one you could choke on.

8

What time is it? How much of that sticky, elastic stuff has passed? And how much is left?

If it appears in this languid meander that all the world's watches have stopped, that nothing is happening or ever can happen, that the universe, for mysterious reasons or none at all, is holding its breath, then I have managed to convey exactly my own impression of having been caught in amber.

This procession will never end. Like the Chinese army, they will march past our reviewing stand forever in their interminable regiments and battalions, having plenty of time to replenish themselves by reproducing, even with the severe restrictions the People's Republic has laid upon them of one child per household. A dismaying prospect, is it not? An inexhaustible supply of young lawyers, marching forth to do battle in their offices and our courtrooms.

Our society has seen an increase in the number of lawyers that is without precedent in recorded history. If the trend continues, there will come a time, in only a generation or two, when everyone in the country will be a lawyer. One hundred percent of the population will have been admitted to the bar. Or maybe there will be one poor contrarian fellow who will refuse, if only out of public-mindedness, so that someone can be the client.

But this is assuming that the passage of time resumes and that the works of the world's constipated clocks are adjusted so that the ticking recommences. Or, to change the figure, let us imagine a droplet of water that has gathered at the lip of a faucet and impends over the sink. There had been a slow drip, but a turn of the spigot interrupted it and the flow of water stopped. But still, that last globule, holding on by the complicated physics of surface tension and ignoring the pull of gravity's law, looms over the porcelain abyss, figuring dramatically not only the cessation of the Bergsonian *durée* but also Coleridge's willing – or should he have put it more strongly and said "willful"? – suspension of disbelief.

How long will that tremulous droplet hang there?

But the question in that form necessarily misrepresents the truth of the situation. It isn't that the droplet is persisting through time but, on the contrary, time itself that is suspended, as the drop of water, having paused, having perhaps found a moment of equilibrium, or more simply out of a disinclination to continue to do the predictable thing, interrupts somehow the motion of the entire universe, which has been depending upon it.

Can it be that because of some quirk in the plumbing here in the men's room, or in an unremarkable building somewhere across town or even across the country, I am caught here forever (as, at least putatively, you are, too, for it begins to seem that this book will go on and on, like *The Man Without Qualities*)?

No, surely not.

A bizarre and dopey idea.

But that doesn't make it untrue, does it?

Anyway, truth, in a novel, is whatever we can agree

on: novels offer the truth of fiction, while history offers the fiction of truth.

Behind the scrim of the fiction, however, there will some-times be the discernible outlines of the stagehands who come on to lug furniture onto the set for the next scene, and we all know, without having to discuss it, that while the actors are acting, these people are merely behaving. It would be an outrageous violation of the proprieties if one of the stagehands were to turn, face the audience, and address us with whatever was on his mind …

What it would do, of course, would be to turn the stagehands into actors, which would mean that they'd have to join another union.

It is an interesting device for some playwright to explore, perhaps, but we may, in the meantime, entertain ourselves by considering not only the differences between the two groups of people on stage but also, and perhaps more interestingly, their similarities. Their hours are roughly the same and their checks are made out by the same payroll clerk, for they are engaged, after all, in the same enterprise.

Stephen and Leo are brothers, because brotherhood is what holds out the promise of mutual affection and con-sideration that is, more often than not, broken and betrayed, as we read, over and over again, in the Bible stories. If their subject is the fatherhood of God and the brotherhood of man, the pieties of family life are violated again and again. I have been trying not to think about Belgium.

I have been trying not to think about my sister, who is not here and whose absence is almost as oppressive to me as Nina's presence. These ceremonies are milestones, occasions upon which the weary traveler may look back to consider how he has lived and see how far he has come. I remember how, when Malcolm was born and I held him for the first time, I thought how healthy he was, how the tissues are all starting out new, and sound, and vigorous, and how there was inevitably a moral dimension to that: the innocence of the newborn is a persuasive idea, even though very few newborns bother their heads about it. The idea is one that we hold on to, more aware than at other times of our defects and shortcomings, and regretting them bitterly.

Malcolm? What kind of name is that?

It's what Nina wanted. The baby was being named after her grandfather, Meshullam, which is perhaps a heavy burden for an American kid to carry, but I liked it anyway. It was, you will agree, an impressive mouthful.

And Malcolm? That was Scottish, with tartans and bagpipes, sporrans and steaming platefuls of haggis …

He's used to it now, I guess.

I'm not. I should have fought harder.

To be peaceable, I gave in.

Meshullam, of course, means peaceable.

It would have been a year and a half ago when Malcolm told me that there was a possibility of his doing an internship in Washington at the Federal Trade Commission. No money, of course, which is how internships work, but it was a smart investment to make in his career. And it would not only cost him to live there for the ten weeks, but there would be the money that he wasn't going to be making at a summer job.

He'd had a series of horrible jobs in the summer, sordid and unseemly employment that he accepted because it was remunerative. He did telephone surveys. Or sold time-shares. He never complained and even pretended that it was amusing to be insulted and to have people hang up on him.

I admired him for what he did and how he did it, and was grateful that he never reproached me for not being able to cough up more money that would have spared him some of these dreadful and depressing encounters. Even when he told me about the internship, he just mentioned it as a possibility: there was no pressure on me to kick in more than I could afford.

Of course, I wanted to help as much as I could. And one of the ideas I had was that he could save a considerable amount of money if he stayed with my sister, his Aunt Alice, who lives in the District and whose children have left the nest, so that she has two bedrooms she doesn't use.

It wouldn't have been much of an imposition. In the summertime, she's away most weekends. And during the week, she and Harvey, my brother-in-law, both work until seven or eight every evening. They'd actually see Malcolm for maybe twenty minutes a week. He would not be imposing much. And, anyway, what are families for?

I called Alice. And she said no. She said she and Harvey "needed their space," which might have had some psychological dimension to it, or could have been just meaningless jargon. Or maybe it had no meaning at all. Maybe these were the words that popped into her head that sounded a little less deplorable than an unadorned "No."

I suppose I could have argued. I could have reproached her. When had I ever asked her for anything before? What kind of family is it where you turn away your brother's child? Would our mother and father have behaved this way? What would our grandparents have done? Didn't she remember the stories we'd heard when we were young of second cousins appearing from darkest Poland to sleep on the floor of our grandfather's shop until they could find a job and a room of their own?

The receiver had turned to lead, had become unimaginably heavy. I could not hold it a moment longer. I watched in detached interest as it lowered itself to the cradle.

Malcolm said it didn't really matter. And he said he was sorry, as if he'd done something wrong.

I didn't believe him. And even if it didn't matter to him, it mattered to me.

That was the last time I talked to my sister.

❖

You can divorce a wife, or she can divorce you. But with a sister or brother, you're stuck. There are no courts that can issue a decree to dissolve that bond. The relationship continues in its ghostly and negative way, the absence of the other sibling taking on a set of characteristics and becoming a low-level presence.

The weekend is when I don't call her, but the prompting remains, the way an ex-smoker will feel the call of the nicotine at moments when cigarettes used to be a part of life's routines. I look at the phone and, as often as not, remember, for a brief moment, the weight the receiver had in my hand and its descent into the cradle. And the silence afterwards, because I couldn't quite believe what had happened and was all but certain that the device would ring, that she would call back, angry perhaps that I had hung up on her, or contrite because, after only the briefest consideration, she realized that she had done an unimaginably terrible thing …

But the instrument was as mute as if it had been unplugged from the wall. As if the wires connecting us had been cut.

"It's quiet out there. Too quiet," they say in the movies, and a horse nickers, and we all know that the Comanches are about to come streaming down from the hillcrest, whooping and hollering. Or, worse than that, the silence will simply extend itself for months, for years.

9

There is applause, that peal of it we had been asked to hold, as if it were urine. All the graduates and honorees together we now acknowledge – unless in a moment of candor, which is untoward in such proceedings (not only untoward but positively froward), what some of us are clapping about is that the exercises are over. Or almost over. There are still some concluding remarks by the chancellor, and the benediction by the not-too-denominational clergyman.

A classmate of mine reported to me that his son married a young woman of another faith, and that after some strenuous hunting around, they found "the minister of them all," unless, of course, it was "the Minister of the Mall." My classmate never had the nerve, or the heart, to inquire.

"Tmesis," I told him.

"Is that a religion?" he asked.

To some of us, yes, I should have said, but didn't.

The applause is not for my restraint on that occasion. Instead, as I allow myself to imagine, and, indeed, more than half believe, it is for me and a few fellow sufferers who have been alone with our thoughts in this foretaste of one of the more persuasive representations of hell. We have, miraculously enough, survived. Which means that it wasn't hell after all, but only purgatory.

It is also possible that the applause is simply for the resumption of the passage of time. The droplet has dropped, the interruption of the processes of the universe has ended almost as unimaginably as it began, and we are as happy as we ever get to have been returned to our familiar array of griefs and torments. Steve and Leo will return to their family squabbles in their usual haunts and leave me with my own, which are less entertaining. And Lumpka and Blooma?

Ah, lovely Lumpka and beautiful Blooma! I shall miss them with their babushkas and dirndls, their politically incorrect accents, and their stolid certainty that, whatever sordidness and catastrophe attended them, they were invincibly in the right. They were dreadful little cartoon figures, but cartoon characters can transcend their moral defects and endear themselves to us. We are less forgiving in real life, and least able to tolerate the failings of our own flesh and blood.

In those days immediately following the rupture, after she had refused to house her nephew for the summer (assuming of course that he was able to get the internship), I remembered the business with the mousse, which was not, I deeply regret to say, imaginary. Unlike Leo and Lumpka, I did not attack the mousse in Alice's refrigerator with my bare hands. I used the usual utensils. It was my sister's house, and I assumed that if I was hungry I could help myself to whatever was there in the refrigerator. Lumpka's reassurances? There was never even a question to which answers had to be supplied.

But the mousse was for the guests who were coming that evening, and the circle of fish was no longer perfect and pristine. By helping myself even to a little bit of it, I had reduced Alice's offering to ordinary food, or, indeed, to leftovers. Thoughtless? Sure, I'll plead to that. In a literal way, I just didn't think. And I can even imagine Alice being annoyed with me. But for her to be angry and for her to tell me that she was angry …

She came back from her dinner party, and I came back from the evening of speeches and glad-handing that had brought me to Washington, and she told me that I'd embarrassed her. She had had to scoop the mousse into a bowl and … And it was just terrible.

I told her it didn't sound so terrible to me. What was terrible was that I was her brother and that she was speaking to me this way.

She didn't see it. I didn't see how she couldn't see it. I went upstairs, repacked my suitcase, and went out to the car to drive back to New York. At one in the morning, actually.

Outrageous!

But after a month or so, I'd cooled down. And we patched things up, somehow.

But that affront had been to me, and that was tolerable. Her refusal to put Malcolm up was different and was beyond any forgiveness I could ever imagine.

Because I already felt guilty about Malcolm and how the failure of my marriage to Nina had driven him to hide underneath that building at school where, in the darkness and the earthy redolence, he must have been able to imagine something like the peace of the grave.

That he was able eventually to recover and get on with his life doesn't diminish the encounter. I have always supposed that Lazarus, after his revival, carried with him some taint of cerecloth. His investment in what we take to be the realities of life, the daily round of work and sleep, must have been less than wholehearted. And to his friends and neighbors, and relatives, too, he must have seemed a stranger, holy, wonderful, but disturbing.

Malcolm has been like that, for me.

And the grief and rage that well up in me whenever I think about Malcolm and my sister are large, genocidal, Bosnian, Central African. All those mass graves of Kosovars and Rwandans are evidence of the pitch of hatred to which human beings can be brought. Such hatred is disgraceful. Or, as they would answer if they were given the opportunity, to feel such bitter hatred and not do anything about it is a disgrace.

Still, there is something that is not only disgusting but also thrilling in the idea of the Serbian security forces digging up the rotting cadavers of the ethnic Albanians they'd slaughtered and bringing them to the furnace of a conveniently situated lead smelting plant to keep the evidence of their war crimes from the NATO troops who were about to arrive.

But didn't Slobodan Miloševic's commanders then feel obliged to slaughter these functionaries, who knew too much and were almost as dangerous as those heaps of corpses?

As we get higher up on the chain of command, at each level, there would be fewer survivors who, if dragged off to testify at The Hague, could inculpate their superiors. The principle is the same as that of musical chairs, although the stakes are higher. And the elegant part is that at every round, because the guilt is greater, there would be less cause for compunction.

Never mind the rule of law. The law of rule is that executives execute.

10

"We ask your blessing, O Lord, on the graduates here today, and on their teachers, and most especially on their loving parents," the Minister of the Mall intones.

Behind him, the Voivod sits in his scarlet academic robes, smiling at this mockery of European pieties. Meanwhile, a few blocks away on the Rue l'Oeuflau, in the subbasement of the Secretariat, although there may have been certain changes in personnel, the activity remains much the same as it was in the days of the Nazis or the Communists, with uniformed young men (and, now, accommodating the demands of the NATO representatives for equality of opportunity, young women, too) carrying out their "forceful interrogations" upon which the security of the state depends. Before them, strapped to tables or suspended from doorframes, their pitiable naked subjects shriek or whimper. Many of those interrogators hold a juris doctorate from this very school, where they first learned the art and science of extorting confessions from the uncooperative.

Comes now the deponent who says: Subject admits that he was in the wrong when he helped himself to the salmon mousse. Subject no longer maintains that it was Lumpka's idea, in which he only reluctantly acquiesced, but accepts full responsibility for the violation of the proprieties and the infringement of Stefan's rights. Subject is willing to offer apologies and to make restitution for the harm he did to Stefan, his comrade and brother, and to Blooma, his comrade and sister-in-law. But subject has not yet seen fit to retract his criticism of Stefan and Blooma for their denial of hospitality to his son, Bohuslav, who, having been turned away from the door of their dacha and having lost his way in a snowstorm white-out, froze to death, for which unfortunate occurrence subject holds Stefan and Blooma responsible. Subject persists in his unwillingness to recant and insists on his own interpretation of the events, which he says he will maintain "to his dying breath." He has lost consciousness several times, and attending medical consultants have warned against further interrogation at this time.

Respectfully submitted, Affidavit Gorki.

There is the customary motion that the document may be made part of the record, and Lord Lovaduck raps his gavel and announces, "So ordered."

So the torture continues, which is to say that that longed-for dying breath keeps on not happening. This durance vile extends itself, and I try to maintain a facial expression appropriate to pleasant occasions. No frown. No scowl. But not actually smiling, either, because a smile tends to get too broad, going way beyond satisfaction or approval and verging on idiocy. I had been tempted to duck this, to find some excuse, but Nina is too smart and would have known that, whatever indisposition I had invented, cowardice was the underlying defect. Nina would not even have had to share this suspicion with Jason and Malcolm who, being our sons, would have been sharp enough to suspect me, all by themselves, sua sponte.

Ah, yes, Sweet Sue, Miss Asponte, Lord Lovaduck's humorless, severe, but not unattractive clerk. She has access to the sealed records of the litigants and, for a small lagniappe, will, as a matter of personal conviction and in the name of justice and equity, make them available to any interested parties or even unrelated passersby. Behind any of these beaming faces here at the commencement exercises, there could be regret and chagrin as bitter as mine, pangs as sharp as mine of self-recrimination for having failed as a parent.

That the child survived and prospered doesn't diminish the guilt but actually enhances it, for the sons and daughters who have been crossing the stage to receive their degrees have persevered in spite of our shortcomings and our neglect, which is to say, they deserved better at our negligent hands.

If we could take a look into Ms. Asponte's files, who knows what horrors would emerge? When STASI's dossiers were made public, it turned out that most East Germans were spying on one another. Which means that almost everyone was pretending to be a normal citizen engaged in the usual occupations and preoccupations of living. But then, at night, there would be the sound of typing that would tap and stammer from every squalid flat in the nation, as they all got down to their real work as informants. It was a paranoid's heaven.

As this may well be a depressive's heaven. What have we got? A seventh of the population is on some sort of antidepressant medication. How many do there have to be before medication is declared to be normal and its lack is classified as pathologic? Those who do not take pills would then be classified as chuckleheads, although the clinicians would use a more dignified and probably Greek word.

I am – of course! – evading the question, which is whether I am alone in my misery or have more company than I can imagine. (And is that company comforting or does it reduce the importance of my miseries, which, in that event, would no longer be singular and interesting but merely predictable and banal?) I hope, for the sakes of all those bright young men and women, that they are not burdened, as Malcolm is, with parents on the edge of hysteria and despair, but I fear the worst, because that's what the worst is for, after all.

Is there a sausage maker somewhere who has called his shop The Wurst Case?

I can imagine that we are all sitting here together and that every one of them is as inadequate and as aware of his defects as I am, and all of us are the subjects of the newest and most exquisite refinement of the Chinese water torture, in which, instead of the droplets of water banging down on the forehead of immobile victims, we are forced merely to continue breathing, one terrible inhalation after another. And there is no one to whom we can plead for relief or mercy.

"And let us say, 'Amen,'" the minister concludes.

There is a brisk fanfare and the brass ensemble commences the repetitive recessional, to which the graduates march out while we stand, either in respect or to get a better view. Or simply to stretch. But the breathing continues, the chests' insufferable heaving and the diaphragms' relentless pumping in every one of us, as the hearts perseverate their primitive tattoo and our suffering extends itself further into that bright future of which this is, the tired convention proclaims, only the commencement.

11

Life is the correction to fantasy, which is a problem novelists have to deal with. The extravagant tastelessness of Sarajevo – the concept restaurant – would have been, at least for a little while, amusing. Almost as depressing, and subtler, Bitter Rice is a Chinese restaurant Malcolm patronized in his student days, and it was his choice, of course, as to where to hold the celebratory meal. It is also more than likely, given Malcolm's instinctive thoughtfulness, that he picked it because it was cheap, and I would be picking up the tab.

Nina disapproves. I gathered from her basilisk stare that she was making a series of unkind judgments on the place and on me. She must assume that this is the best I can do, so that Malcolm's thoughtfulness, without anyone saying a word, gets turned around, and his choice of restaurant turns nasty and demeaning, an occasion for insult and scorn. Nina has a talent for ringing such changes on the transactions of ordinary life. Bitter Rice, indeed.

Basilisk is, perhaps, on the menu, although it may not show up on the English side of the page. I have always imagined that they keep the good stuff – the rhino horn soup, the panda lips, and other such delicacies – for themselves. What we get offered is never more exotic than General Li's chicken, which is, presumably, a northern, Yan Kee dish.

What I'm saying, of course, is that this wouldn't have been my choice, however modest in cost. I'd have been willing to splurge a little. But Malcolm has his odd ideas about "authenticity," which is not what you expect from a young lawyer, but who knows what they're like these days?

Malcolm, Jason, Caroline, who is Jason's wife, Nina, Allen, who is Nina's husband, Joanne, who is Malcolm's girl- friend, and me. At one of those big round tables for eight with a lazy Susan in the middle of it. The eighth chair, the one beside me, is trebly empty. Nina and I are divorced. With Samantha, who was the occasion of the breakup of my marriage to Nina, I have also broken up. Or off. Or down. So, she's not there either. And my sister Alice, who could have occupied the empty seat, is also absent – at my request. Malcolm was willing to invite her or not – as I preferred. As if it were my quarrel. (As, of course, it is.)

So, to my right is the empty chair. In which Nachman of Bratslav sits, presiding, even though dead, over his Chasidim. Or Elijah. Or the ghost of Christmas past. Or it's the Siege Perilous in which no Galahad will ever take his place. To my left is Caroline, who is terminally nice. It is difficult to decide what put her here. Either her instinc- tive niceness prompted her to choose this chair next to the pariah, or else, in an ostensibly casual and offhand way, Nina could have suggested that she might put herself next to me, not saying – not having to say – that this would spare everyone else.

Which of these dismal possibilities would I find more distressing, and therefore more likely? It is not easy to decide.

"It was a nice commencement," she says to me, demonstrating that, however the rest of the family may behave, she is going to talk to me, or at least is going to acknowledge my presence. But, my God! I can imagine her in Kosovo nodding that way, as if to prompt agreement from a not very bright interlocutor as she says, "It was a nice massacre," or "It was a nice mass burial."

I am being unfair. She is not a fool, after all, and is uncomfortable. Very probably, she may have some notion that I may be uncomfortable, too, which she is likelier than most people to find distressing. So she is making an effort, however awkward, to dispel the awkwardness or at least cover it over.

"Very nice," I agree. And for all I know, it might have been. How would I know? I caught only a few random moments of it.

Her relentless pleasantness is perhaps contagious? It occurs to me that Jason may have been attracted to her precisely because she is always so calm, so cheerful, so determined to put the best possible face on things. He may have been too old to hide under school buildings the way Malcolm was doing, but he, too, would have felt some pain at the death of the family, and in Caroline's niceness he could well have seen a possible refuge. That what she says is so unrealistic as to risk stupidity could be, in his eyes, pardonable.

Isn't this putting the best face on things? And how far am I willing to go in this sappy direction? There must be some limit. Can she find something to approve of about this restaurant? And if she does, will I nod along with her, and smile back at her smile, and agree that, yes, it, too, is very nice. Wonderful place. Fine place. A really good place to come to eat your heart out. Or to eat crow. And the humble pie is very good, too.

She would not approve of such jokes. She would find them unhelpful. She might even express herself in the strongest terms available in her limited vocabulary of criticism, in which, with great provocation, she may admit that she doesn't "appreciate" something. And I shouldn't be at all surprised if Malcolm were to realize that he shares his brother's preferences. Joanne, whose presence here may or may not be significant, could turn out to be as cheerful and agreeable as Caroline, but she is so quiet that it's difficult to tell. At least she doesn't nod all the time.

These are folkways that are foreign to me, as exotic as the behaviors of those Melanesians I always hoped the anthropologists might have invented. Who, after all, was likely to go out to their remote atolls, paddle over their treacherous reefs in a picturesque but not reliably seaworthy outrigger canoe, and brave the cannibals and headhunters just to check up on whatever combination of truth and fantasy some desperado academic had dispatched in the hope of a promotion to associate professor?

It's Bronislaw Malinowski I'm thinking of, I guess, but for him the habits of the islanders in Britain would have been quaint and curious. If you grow up under the grisaille of Krakow, the rest of the world looks unlikely, the sun too bright, the skies too blue, and the grass too green. For him, the first anthropological exploration would have been in London, after which the Trobriand Islanders would have been just another collection of mild eccentrics who didn't speak Polish. Their society, their system of totems and taboos, their matrilineal tribal organization, their unpredictable combination of savagery and gentleness would have been interesting, at least at first, but also arbitrary and whimsical.

And if that's the case, why limit one's reports to what they're doing, this bunch of ignorant coconut eaters with paint on their faces and feathers in their hair? Why not embellish? It would be easy enough to imagine improvements or even to invent as interesting a culture out of whole cloth, which would promote the diffident scholarly Pole from mere reporter to author, which is to say, god.

The notion came to him when he showed them how he could kindle fires by focusing the rays of the sun through one of the lenses of his spectacles. They assumed he was some sort of shaman or magician or priest. Or perhaps even a god. They didn't speak Polish and he had to guess at what their grunts and whistles meant, but clearly they were suggesting that he partook somehow of the sacred. It was an idea that was flattering and difficult to resist, and it prompted the further thought – how much fun he could have had, lying on a hammock, nibbling the breadfruit tidbits they brought him, and dreaming up what it was they might be doing, or ought to have been doing all along.

Matrilineal, obviously, but what happens when you ask your sister to take your son into her village, where the fishing is said to be better? She turns him away, of course, because, properly, he's his mother's responsibility. As you have become your ex-wife's mother's charge – which is a calculatedly precarious position for a man to be in. (This is how the wily Trobrianders have devised a disincentive for divorce.)

The rare male who so much as voices an objection to this dispensation is banished from the island and, as a punishment for his disregard of the rule of law, "sent north," which is the delicate euphemism for the death sentence: he is set adrift in one of those outrigger canoes with only a couple of coconuts and a small knife – with which he can either bone the occasional fish he may be lucky enough to catch or, alternatively, to use it to slash his wrists or throat. But it doesn't matter to them. He's out of sight and out of mind.

Once in a great while, one of these exiles will come sneaking back onto the island, but he is shunned. No one speaks to him, not even his own children, or their otherwise pleasant and cheerful wives. He lurks like a ghost around their campfire trying to snatch a mouthful of food whenever he can, but food is never the issue in that lush tropical setting. It is the psychological burden that eventually breaks him so that, after a time, he returns voluntarily to the sea, either in the canoe or, if he is clever, just swimming out toward the horizon so that he may have a quicker and less agonizing death.

But, Professor, does no one ever become violent?

Violence is not part of their culture. They are not hunters but fishermen and gatherers of fruit. They are as pacific as the ocean in which they make their home.

Pacific. Peaceable. Meshullam.

"Are you all right?" Caroline asks. Her expression is hard to read. Concern? Or is it fear?

"Yes, of course. Why do you ask?"

"You seem to be … weeping," she says, getting the word out even though it goes very much against her grain.

"Am I?" I put my hand up to my cheek and, yes, find that rivulets of tears have trickled down the sides of my nose. I rub them away.

"I'm happy," I tell her. "I'm happy for Malcolm and proud of him."

That last part, anyway, is true.

❖

I was wrong, of course. Those ghostly creatures do not disappear or go for the long swim, however appealing that prospect might sometimes seem. Instead, they stay, lurking presences, all but invisible – as I seem to be, sometimes – but capable nonetheless of a love from which it is impossible to turn away. Their children, on whom they came to spy and from whom they cannot now escape, cannot see them or hear them, but they are sometimes aware of a liveliness in the air, as of swarms of midges. They may, if they are acute enough, even have an eerie sense, now and then, of being observed. And, to put the matter in the best possible light, I may allow myself to suppose that over time they come to accept the company of these familiar wraiths, grow accustomed to them and think of them as normal. To be without them would be to be diminished.

I wonder if I am as much a part of Malcolm's experience of this day as Steve and Leo and Lumpka and Blooma have been of mine.

"You're very quiet over there," Nina says. She shows the same kind of concern that a Serbotian interrogator might exhibit when a torture victim fails to respond.

"Yes," I agree. "I'm just taking it all in," I tell her. That is not true, of course. I'm taking in much less than all. As much as I can bear, perhaps, but by no means all.

And then, because they are all looking at me and I see a way of retrieving the moment gracefully, I add, "I was just telling Caroline how happy I am for Malcolm, and how proud of him. And I was thinking that I ought to tell that to Malcolm, as well."

A part of me realizes that the least desirable outcome she could have imagined would be just this kind of pleasant, civilized exchange. Another part of me is aware that, whatever the pressures and stresses of the occasion, what I find myself saying is right and the truth. I hold up my teacup. "To Malcolm. Congratulations. Success. And happiness."

One is not supposed to toast with water, but the prohibition does not extend, I think, to tea.

The others hold up their teacups to Malcolm, joining in the toast. Joining me. For us ghosts at the campfire, this is a rare and wonderful moment.

Malcolm holds up his teacup and responds, "To all of you, I thank you for coming," he says. But he is looking at me.

We all take a ceremonial sip of the tea that is by now lukewarm, Jason, Caroline, Nina, Allen, Joanne, and I. And my friends, Steve and Leo. And Mina and Mona and Sam. They come on to take a curtain call with the supers and bit-players like P. Kabou and Doris and lazy Sue Asponte, who even now is doing a turn in the middle of the table and serving whoever will give her a whirl. Even absent Alice is wishing me well. They all applaud, proud of Malcolm for having done so well, and proud of me, too.

I have surprised them, and myself most of all, by getting through this. I have not, at any rate, disgraced myself. I have not let anyone know that I am hurting. What they suppose, they suppose, but I have given them no new ammunition.

I signal to the waiter and get the check. Nina and Allen will be going back to Jason and Caroline's house and will have dinner there with Malcolm and Joanne. I was invited, too, but only after a heated discussion I have tried not to imagine, in which Jason had to insist to his mother that she could not, on an occasion like this, exclude me from his house. She backed down, finally. And, having been invited, I could thank him and decline, knowing that this would make his life lots easier. And Malcolm's. And mine, too, of course.

Jason and Malcolm tried to conceal their relief, but I told each of them what they knew anyway – that it would be better all around if we got together some other time.

So I pay the bill, I kiss Malcolm and Jason, and I walk out into the bright May sunshine, a painful dazzle that proclaims itself as reality.

"Sufficient unto the day is the evil thereof," says Adage Gorki, to which the Imam of Oman replies, "Amen."

And I am able to conclude the ceremony, saying Go in peace. Meshullam.

II. Ice Capades

1

Although the appearance in a novel of a Roman numeral can suggest the passage of time, the fact that clock faces often sport Roman numerals is a mere coincidence. But then, in novels, are coincidences ever merely mere? Are they not, more likely than not, manifestations of the workings of fate? The author – of the book? of the universe? – has, for just a moment, shown his hand, and in that glimpse we can suppose we have seen through to the secret core of things. At least for the time being, we feel that we are not altogether helpless and mystified, but have some notion of how life works and can hope that we are therefore better equipped to face its challenges.

No one comes out and says this directly, because it is patently absurd and would be rejected instanter by any reader intelligent enough for an author to want to claim. But that's how it is, isn't it? Or how it used to be, back when the novel wasn't, in itself, an awkwardness. Once upon a time, "Once upon a time" was not a set-up for a joke.

Who believes in novels anymore? What is interesting – even wonderful – is that they survive, nevertheless, as prayer books of a religion in which we may have lost faith and from which we are apostates, but for which we retain some sentimental attachment. Could Nietzsche have supposed that after the death of god, Santa Claus would survive and even thrive? And Rudolph the red-nosed reindeer?

We read novels, reverting or resorting to them sometimes, but mostly from nostalgia. One could say that we bring fictive selves to the encounter with fiction so that the encounter, itself, is also a fiction. And at this dance of shadows' shadows, we notice a certain anemia, which we resent because we realize it is our fault as much the author's.

My shadows, however, these dream figments that bedevil me, are not at all anemic but full of life and menace. I have learned, at any rate, to fear them. They appear without having been summoned, romp and cavort in deplorable abandon, and refuse to go away when I try to dismiss them.

Sanity, I sometimes think, is no more than the ability to keep other people from suspecting what is going on in one's head.

Marty is dead. His demise was not unexpected: he was ninety-two and had been in fragile health for some time. And my relationship to him was tenuous, almost fictional, but it was a fiction to which both of us acceded. There isn't even a convenient word for an ex-father-in-law, only that awkward portmanteau phrase, *Le parapluie de mon beau-père ancien est dan le portmanteau*. Still, we had managed to maintain at those family gatherings where we encountered each other a degree of civility that did us both credit – but him more than me. I had expected him to honor the ties of blood, take his daughter's part, and, for her sake as much as his own, despise me. He may even have had, from time to time, feelings of animosity toward me. But he concealed them. He always behaved well. He displayed a generosity and even an affability and charm that I came to value for its rarity. I was still his grandchildren's father, after all.

A few days before he died, we spoke on the phone. Malcolm had kept me informed about his failing health, and, thinking of how well Marty had behaved and how grateful I was, I'd decided to brave calling Nina in order to speak to him one last time, to acknowledge his kindness, and, *tout court*, say good-bye.

I told him I was sorry to hear that he was under the weather. (Ah, that *parapluie*, which it is unlucky to open in the house!) Marty responded with similar understatement, saying that he'd been better. Then there were a couple of breaths while I tried to think of what else to say, because it was my turn. That's the way conversations go, after all. A says something and then B says something. And then A replies … But what I was thinking was that we were both breathing, and his breathing was soon going to stop. And one couldn't allude to that.

"Jason and Caroline are down there?" I said. I knew perfectly well that my son and daughter-in-law had gone down for the deathwatch. But it was something to say.

"Yes," Marty said. "They've been helpful. He's a good boy. You should be proud of him."

"I am. He's turned out well."

"They both have," he said, behaving well even now, for quite possibly what he was telling me was that he did not resent Malcolm's absence.

And then it was my turn. (Why hadn't I thought more about this before I'd called, made a couple of notes even?)

"I've been thinking about you," I managed at last, the pressure of the moment forcing me to risk violating the convention of understatement we seemed to have accepted.

"I've been thinking about you, too," he said. I didn't disbelieve him, exactly, but it crossed my mind that the quality of those thoughts had been left unspecified. But, as if he had guessed what I might be thinking, he went on to specify. "You should know that I've always liked you. Liked you and loved you."

"I love you, too," I said.

A breath, another, and then he said, "Thanks for call-ing." And he hung up, which saved him from having to hear my sudden, unimpeachably sincere, and not at all under-stated sobbing.

I was not invited to the funeral. Jason actually had to convey to me his mother's preference that I not attend. But then I asked him to ask Nina whether she'd object if I appeared at the cemetery for the interment. Maybe thirty percent of that was calculated to be annoying, to let her know that I thought I had a right to be there and to establish that my absence would be entirely her responsibility. The rest of it was what it should have been in its entirety – an honest desire to pay my respects.

Jason reported back to me that Nina supposed it was okay; I could come if I felt I had to.

In other words, it was as grudging and supposititious a yes as she could devise. But it still meant that I had to go. A two-hour drive each way. And to a formal family occasion of the kind that I find troublesome, even when they are happy.

So who won?

It wasn't about Marty anymore. Marty, remember, was dead. And insofar as we are able to tell, the dead don't much care what we do or say – even though we may imagine them and pretend that they are looking down at us, approving or disapproving the choices we have made, beaming or spinning in their graves. We may not erect family shrines or offer up Shinto prayers, but we nonetheless invoke our dead in order to please them or to appease them when we have behaved badly, and to promise that we will do better next time.

What's the harm? None whatever, except that the practice turns each life into a fiction, subordinating external reality or, at the very least, putting it in quotation marks that inevitably raise some question as to the reliability of the narrator-protagonist. For the sake of our remote forebears on the Field of Blackbirds, we will kill ethnic Albanians or Serbs, or ... (fill in the blank). These are hate crimes, which is what we call crimes of passion when we disapprove of the passion. They are as likely as not to be crimes of pride, and therefore of love, however distorted and perverse.

What made Leopold II such a monster was that his crimes in the Congo, unprecedented at the time for their brutality, were motivated merely by greed and indifference, and therefore were much more unspeakable. He looms behind Joseph Conrad's *Heart of Darkness*, but students who read that book now have to be told who he was. The world forgets, and Brussels is now the capital of Europe, representing itself as the center of civility and enlightenment (even though, as I recall, the Belgian government was nearly brought down a few years ago because of a scandal about politicians involved in pornography and child prostitution).

In a way, that miserable little king of the sprouts was worse than Hitler, who may have been crazy but at least had an ideology, however repulsive, to justify what he was doing. Leopold, altogether rational, acted out of mere personal greed, killing and enslaving the people of the Congo and ruining the land. For rubber. For francs.

President Mobutu once said that he admired Leopold II because he was "a strong man," and when he fled the country with as much swag as he could carry, he bought a villa on the Riviera within sight of another villa that had once been owned by Leopold II.

Mobutu died a few months later, a Rimbaud in reverse.

My failure to appear at the graveside would be a demonstration of indifference. It would be cowardly not to go. But then, I have to admit that it is cowardice that drives me, because I want to avoid the pangs of guilt I'd feel if I didn't.

If only there were such a creature driving me. And without my summons, he springs into being, an obliging fellow named Coward, who simply appears, Johnny on the spot, as soon as he's thought of and as happy to act as chauffeur as if he had been created for just that purpose (as, of course, he was). He has an apologetic smile for his joke name, and, in a beautifully tailored black suit, crisp white shirt, black tie, and visored cap, he is holding the door for me, and then getting in behind the limousine's wheel for the long haul to the bury patch.

Do I call him Johnny? Or would we both be more comfortable if I were to address him by his last name, *à l'Anglaise*? The latter, I think.

If I were to appear this way, Nina would be horrified, which would be fine. It could even be a kindness to distract her from her grief by giving her something to disapprove of, aside, of course, from my mere existence. It'd be almost worth the money to hire a limo and a driver just to do that.

But the boys would think I was being contentious. And disrespectful.

Sorry, Coward, another time perhaps.

"Yaas, boss," he says, sounding a bit gravelly, like Charlie Chan's Manton Moreland or Jack Benny's Rochester.

It's the worst of all possible worlds. He won't do the driving; he'll just come along, sit in the back seat of my Toyota, and make wise-ass remarks that I will no doubt have deserved.

No man is a hero to his servants.

Who said that? Not Lenin, surely, nor even Cherny-chevsky, but some clever Frenchman. Not Rimbaud, of course. Nor Francis Ponge, either, although it's closer to his tessitura. (He was the fellow who said that one of the good things about being king is that you never have to touch a doorknob.)

Montaigne, maybe? Madame de Sévigné? Madame Cornuel!

Even though I've just invented him, Coward and I go back a long way, which is, as creationists keep insisting, a part of the game of creating things. You can create histo-ries, too. The Paleozoic monsters are just a kind of back-story God thought it would be diverting to impose on us, to test our faith.

In just that way, Coward is a faithful family retainer, a little-league Leporello, whose subservience is an act that fools neither of us and that he maintains more out of pro-fessional pride than for my sake. Carefully, he adjusts the cuffs of his black trousers so as not to ruin them as he stretches out in the back seat. I should do that, I guess, when I'm back there, but I don't. And he is letting me know that he's noticed. And, although he is too punctilious ever to have mentioned it to me, he disapproves. (Of course, he does. What else would I expect of a figment of mine?)

"Across Staten Island?" I ask him.

"You're the boss, boss. And the driver."

"You're in the back seat," I tell him.

"Just for the ride, boss. It wasn't my call."

"I know," I say. "Look, I'm asking for your advice. Is that how you'd go?"

"It's either that or crossing Manhattan, boss."

"Is that a yes?"

"You could take it that way," he says, meaning either the remark or the drive. In either case, it's across Staten Island and into Brooklyn, and then on to the necropolis out on the island.

2

A monumentally ugly stretch of landscape, this is, what with the abandoned factories and warehouses and the oil refineries of New Jersey, then the enormous landfill on Staten Island, and then the cemeterial sprawl of Long Island. Every prospect pleases, Pope wrote, and only man is vile. But given half a chance, man will wreck the prospect, too, tainting it and bringing it down with him.

I remember seeing in a kindlier light this part of the world through which I have been driving for years now. I used to suppose that these outsized utilitarian structures were healthy manifestations of American muscle. But their utility is no longer self-evident: the refineries are sinister now, and many of those big chemical and paint plants, polluting and inefficient, have been abandoned.

They speak to me still, but differently, more intimately and with a sweet sadness, for we know each other's secrets. My utility is not self-evident anymore either, and I, too, have been abandoned.

It's not nice to say so, but that doesn't make it less true. That sense of having been abandoned is, in fact, one of the threads that runs through the dark tangle of our emotions whenever someone we love dies. We, who outlive him, may be said to have "survived," as if life were a marathon dance contest. But it is just as true that we are among those he "left." Even the most faithful leave eventually, and if we survive, we are nonetheless wounded and diminished.

Marty wasn't my father but merely my father-in-law, my *beau-père*. One need not have spent much time on the couch, however, to see one's way through to the connection. He was a father figure and, now that he is gone, there is no one left of that generation standing between me and the abyss. Even if I no longer have any claim on him, it is still true that my children have lost their last grandparent. Through them, then, and on my own, too, I feel a difference.

I am not, practically speaking, at any greater risk than I was last week or last month. His passing has hardly any practical consequence to me. But our emotions do not arise from tawdry practicalities. The *primitif* within each of us believes in an orderly universe we are too embarrassed to acknowledge, in which the angel of death is reasonable or at least respectful of the proprieties so that, when he has

to take someone, he chooses from members of the appropriate cohort. It is as if we imagined him as some sort of
sport angler who threw back fish that were too small. By
this reckoning, which is, I admit, altogether stupid, Marty's
longevity was an achievement that was of interest and benefit to Nina and Ronald, her brother. And to my children.
And not inconceivably to me, too.

Or to put it another way, there was, mixed in with my
sense of loss at Marty's death, a reprise of my bereavement
at the death of my own father.

"You don't want to go there, boss," Coward warns me.
He is a back-seat driver, a coward, and a nuisance. He is
nonetheless correct.

To conflate him with my father would be imprecise and
sentimental. On the other hand, to deny any legitimate
association between them would also be to falsify, erring
the other way in the direction of unfeelingness. Marty was
always more than decent to me, and of how many people
can we say that in the end when we reckon up accounts?
The idea of Judgment Day is a metaphor for the kind of
calculation each of us makes at the end of any life that has
touched our own. And it is not irrelevant that he and my
father, quite different kinds of men, were friendly enough.

My father, I am afraid, was just a little condescending.
After all, he was a lawyer, a professional person, and Marty
was merely "in trade" – a phrase my father used as if we
were landed gentry and rode to hounds. Marty must have
noticed but never showed any annoyance about it. He
indulged this foible of my father's as if he had calculated
that there were worse defects to be expected in one's child's
in-laws. That was how it seemed to me at the time, although

now it appears rather different, and I find myself wondering whether Marty knew somehow that he was destined for such longevity and understood that he could afford to put up with temporary inconveniences because of his serene confidence that he would outlast so many of them.

Certainly, he outlasted my parents. And three of his own wives. He floated through life, a dapper dresser, a suave and attractive fellow whose odd hobby was ballroom dancing, which I thought was silly but which was exactly the right kind of moderate exercise to keep him limber, supple, and remarkably fit well into his late eighties. He tangoed, cha-cha-ed, and rumba-ed his way through the whole of that difficult decade, not even pausing to mop his brow with the elegantly folded handkerchief he sported in the pocket of his camelhair blazer as he defied the menace of age and infirmity and, with grace and bravery, delighted the sprightlier widows of Florida's Gold Coast.

It is impossible even to imagine my father executing any step more complicated than a fox trot or a relatively decorous waltz.

The Verrazano Bridge is high and wide enough, but somehow shabby, in a state of disrepair that seems to come less from exposure to the elements or sheer age – it isn't all that old – than from its location, as if some contagion of Brooklyn's squalor and Staten Island's seediness had infected it. And the traffic patterns are deceptive and treacherous. Crossing from Staten Island, one must bear right to go left and head west, or left to turn right and east. The concentration that this requires of me is not without its beneficial effect, for I am at least temporarily distracted from my inner turmoil. For several minutes, I have been untroubled by my apprehension about the interment and have been worried simply about taking the wrong exit ramp.

"You got lotsa time, boss," Coward counsels.

I don't answer, hoping that I may perhaps discourage him. He may leave me alone for a while or even disappear.

But I don't have to answer for him to know what I'm thinking. He's a figment, for God's sake, a part of my own mind, and he therefore knows my mind at least as well as I do. Or better. He lives there, after all, one of the squatters I'd evict if I could.

I've tried, Lord knows, but it's a tricky business. Try not to think about Belgium, and inevitably you're thinking about Belgium. About the Congo. About Leopold and his depredations. Meditation? I've even dabbled in that, in my desperation, and have been able to drive them away for brief periods by concentrating on my breathing. But in the spiritual austerity of silence, as often as not what happens is that I can hear the static more clearly. Under the cover of darkness, they sneak in, like the Achaeans, horsing around with the Trojans.

Beware the gifts of Greeks. *Timeo Danaos et dona ferentes*.

Timmy O'Donahue and Donna Farentis? A couple of ice-skaters is what they sound like, and, voila, there they are, doing their double axels to peppy tunes on the electric organ and sporting their pleading, too-bright smiles and vulgar tinselly costumes in day-glo colors. I can predict for them a minimal success in competitive skating and then a depressing career in the chorus of some ice capade. (No doubt, they can tell as dismal a fortune for me, too, and perhaps are doing just that, if only I could read the hieroglyphs the blades of their skates incise in the ice between visits of the Zamboni machine.)

I breathe slowly, pursing my lips, taking in the good air and forcing out the bad. I cannot make them go away but I can relegate them to the back seat with Coward, where I am resigned to letting the three of them squabble or conspire together as they will.

In the momentary silence, I occupy myself with the cheerful thought that my sister's absence, this time, will be easier to take than at Malcolm's graduation. She and Nina never got on. They detested each other, actually, and, while this used to trouble me, I now find myself inclined to agree with each of them about the other.

I wonder whether Ronald will be there. Will he have the nerve to show up? Or is Nina spiteful enough to try to keep him away even from this?

And then I find myself thinking of Marty and my father and the difference in their responses to disappointment – how, yet again, Marty seemed to waltz through it all, even though he must have been as saddened and as angered with Ronnie as my father was with Alice.

In the back, Timmy and Donna produce from their carry-all a couple of not very convincing rubber masks, which they pull down over their heads, ready to do "Ronnie and Alice" as an ice-capade number.

I am not pleased to have a couple of chucklehead ice-skaters who are ready to morph into a range of characters of what I'd supposed was my life.

"I Morph to See the Wizard," Donna suggests, with a giggle.

I recognize it as tmesis, of course, and pay it no mind.

But why not an ice capade, as easily as a novel or play? Dignity and style have to be earned, don't they?

❖

This buffoonery is distressing, I admit, but the alternative is worse. There are times when, for no discernible reason, I can feel my psyche collapse. It is a sensation akin to being kicked. Whatever the trivial trigger may have been, I am unable to identify it as I feel my precipitous fall into helplessness, hopelessness, and worthlessness. Cognitive therapists claim a mastery over the mystery of these miseries. But their explanations are suspiciously clever, while the experience is both overwhelming and stupid.

I get through it, mostly, by sheer will. March or die, I tell myself, and mostly I am able to drag myself along, if only because of the fear that if I fall behind, a laggard in the sands on the way to Fort Zinderneuf, I will not only perish but, worse yet, just as I am at the point of expiring, vultures will descend from the steely blue of the sky to peck at my still sensitive eyes …

Afrique. Ah, freak! Saharan and sub-Saharan. The heart of its darkness lies within each of us. The quicksands are psychic. The vipers and beasts and B-movie savages are … redundant. Paddling up the dark, gray-green, greasy Limpopo in my tippy dugout canoe (the Tyler II?), I am in as exquisite a distress as Conrad's famous protagonist. And, as they say on late-night television commercials, "in the comfort of my own home."

I have not been kept current about the details of Ronnie's troubles. He came out back before it was politically incorrect to disapprove of such declarations. And before AIDS, too, but that only made it worse, I think. Once the connection between promiscuous sexual activity and HIV had been established, friends, relatives, and even parents could mask their distaste, pretending to a loftier kind of concern that wasn't merely aesthetic or moral but wore the white coat of science. Until then, we had to suppress our envy of all that fun the gays were having. Such good looking guys, and so well and expensively dressed! Not having to worry about providing for children, they could spend whatever they had on themselves.

Or, in Ronnie's case, even what they didn't have. I heard only inadvertent references and vague rumors, but I am persuaded that he has a history of unauthorized borrowings from various employers and clients – he does, or used to do, mysterious things on Wall Street – and that Marty has had repeatedly to bail him out of his difficulties. With money that Nina is convinced her father would otherwise one day have left to her and to our children.

It is not inconceivable that this is one of the considerations that prompted Ronnie to take the risks that he did – assuming of course that any of his actions were in any way considered. My guess would be that, in each instance, he told himself some story about how this was just temporary, promising that he would make good within a few days or a few weeks. Con men can be very persuasive, even to themselves. And after the skiing weekend with the new friend, or the trip to Paris, or whatever it was that had been the proximate cause of his indiscretion, the uptick in the market turned out to be a fantasy. And once you are in a hole of that kind, deeper is the only way to go.

I would almost certainly have disapproved of Ronnie more strenuously if I had been more closely involved. But my only connection with him was through the boys, who, in a very theoretical way, stand now to inherit rather less, assuming that Marty was well off and that he hadn't spent it, and that Nina doesn't. On those rare occasions when we saw each other – weddings, funerals, and maybe bar mitzvahs – Ronnie was charming enough, as con men generally are. And it pleased me to see Nina's anger directed at a target other than myself.

Now that I think of it, I have to assume that the reason for Ronnie's odd invitation to me to join him at Marty's ninetieth birthday party was mostly to annoy Nina, whose expressions of disapproval must have grown tiresome. But that doesn't exclude the possibility that he liked me and that what first prompted the idea was not at all insidious.

Beyond that naughty pleasure I could take in Nina's discomfort with Ronnie's presence, this view I had of the inner workings of a family other than mine was abstractly interesting. In Marty's place, and with lots less cause, my father would have broken off all connection. He might have ponied up money to keep a son out of jail, but he would have been motivated less by concern with the welfare of the child than by an impersonal determination not to allow the family name to be disgraced. We have not had – so far, anyway – convicts rattling their skeletons in our family's closet.

I think of how much less serious Alice's offence was, and how much greater was our father's hurt and rage. The difference, of course, is that the two men had different expectations not only of their children but of the world and how it ought to treat them. Marty was more modest and, I suppose, wiser. My father, on the other hand, had very clear ideas about what the rules were and how people ought to behave. He set a high standard for himself and for the rest of the world, and that may be admirable but it can also be costly. Alice disappointed him and even, by his lights, humiliated him, but nothing she did was illegal or immoral. Still, the blow she inflicted on his *amour propre* ate at his guts, quite literally, and along with his depression he suffered from a colitis that turned at last into the cancer that killed him.

Marty, whose son's behavior was much worse, had a more relaxed view of the world. Or a cast iron stomach and stronger guts. At any rate, he survived.

Weeks can go by when I don't think about Alice at all, but then one of these family rites will come along and I get a sharp twinge, like the phantom pain from an amputated limb. That sounds melodramatic, perhaps, but such pain is, first of all, useless. There is no fire from which to pull the hand back. There is no hand, either, only a neurological fiction, and while the mind may be receiving a physical signal, the discomfort it may bring is less burdensome than the feelings it provokes of hopelessness and grief. And then, blossoming slowly and coloring everything else in the mental landscape, there is an awareness of the irrationality of the entire transaction that impeaches those assumptions on which we have so long relied about the common-sense world.

What is it that the old Belgian doctor recommends to Marlow as the first principle of survival in the tropics? To remain, as far as possible, unperturbed. "Du calme, du calme," he advises. He is something of a nut, with his calipers for cranial measurements, but as the story unfolds, it turns out that he may have been correct. His recommendation is at least as good as any other.

But how do you remain calm when you are driving to your ex-father-in-law's funeral with a cartoon chauffeur named Coward lounging in the back seat, where he is no doubt gossiping about me with a couple of ice-capade stars of the third magnitude? And what is depressing isn't their stupid and malicious chatter but the fact that they have been unable to crowd out Alice's absence.

That was what kept my father company, painfully but intimately, and without let up, for so many years.

It has not been a good year for Timmy and Donna. They tried out for the ice-show version of *Schindler's List* but were offered nothing better than places in the chorus of ice-skating concentration camp inmates, which they declined – although later on they came to regret what may have been a hasty decision. Their agent, Jacques du Calme, was unable to find anything better for them, just a small number in *Goose Bumps*, a nudie ice show that would be on tour in Central and South America. (Even though, as brother Jacques pointed out, Timmy would be wearing a cache-sexe and Donna would be permitted a G string and pasties, she was unenthusiastic.)

I have got to cut this out. They're putting Marty in the ground, and I'm so worried about what terrible things they'll be thinking about me that I'm driven to make up these grotesque and implausible stories. Frère Jacques, indeed! Quelle bêtise! Although, to be more honest than the moment requires, it was Alice I was thinking about not thinking about. To whom else am I the frère?

"You're going in the right direction, boss," Coward tells me. I check in the rearview mirror, but can't see him. He's stretched out on the back seat, then? With Timmy and Donna performing upon him their strenuous and extravagant perversions.

3

On my way through nether Brooklyn, I have been noticing a number of abandoned cars on the side of the road, the first few of which failed to register particularly, but then, as I became aware of them, I realized how many there are. It's as if a civil war has been going on here that the rest of the country doesn't know about. It looks like Kosovo, transplanted. These are not desperate immigrant Kosovars, however, but locals, probably young, displaying the enthusiasm of their generation for unrestrained viciousness. Teen-aged joy-riders, they run out of gas or just get bored, get out of the vehicle they've stolen, and, as an expression of their annoyance and contempt, set it ablaze. Or else they aren't kids but more sinister examples of our society's extravagant waste, so that, in a similar gesture, the owners of these automobiles, perhaps with the insurance in mind, imitate the young culprits in the hope of avoiding, say, the cost of a new rack and pinion.

Speculating about these possibilities, I cannot decide which is worse. It's like the graffito I once saw on the wall at the entrance to a New York subway station: "Fuck the third grade," which could have been written by a third grader ... Or was it a second grader? Or was it perhaps a third-grade teacher?

Such an involuntary unfolding of possibilities, each more disturbing than the one before, can result in an emotional implosion that will stain the entire day. For this reason, I have come to hate and fear my own thoughts, knowing that any one of them might be a trigger for some psychic booby trap. If I am going to be depressed, my feelings ought to have some connection with Marty, to whose burial I am making my way. Why should I care about these derelict automobiles? What have they to do with me?

"You never had a car fire, boss?" Coward asks.

I haven't. But, of course, now I remember that Nina had one. About a month after I moved out. In what had been my car, on the West Side Highway, in stop-and-go traffic, she saw tongues of flame that were coming from under the hood and got out of the car just before the whole engine caught fire.

Hearing this, I felt … relief. But also guilt, because it had been my car and I'd been the one who, in a better run and more orderly universe, ought to have been behind the wheel at that moment. What I'd done, leaving her, was bad enough to merit such punishment, but for her to have the fire…?

There's no such thing as cause and effect. Certainly, there's no heavenly court looking down and deciding who should plummet off the Bridge at San Luis Rey, or should have a car fire on the West Side Highway. We know this, but we don't believe it, because the randomness of the universe is more frightening than even the most capricious Furies we can imagine, who, however inaccurately, allocate according to some general principle the illnesses and catas-trophes that befall us. Knowing better, we look for moral lessons. He got struck by lightning? Zeus must have been angry at him. She had a car fire? Some god must have been pissed off.

I'd offered to come back, after all, to leave Samantha and to come back home. Maybe not with all the enthusi-asm I should have shown, and not for the most romantic reasons. But for the sake of the boys. And because it was the right thing to do. I did make what was a legitimate offer. And she turned me down.

And then, a month later, had a car fire.

Is it possible that all these cars were driven by angry wives whose chastened husbands, for whatever reason, had offered to come home? But they, too, were proud and unbending and they refused, provoking the anger of the gods ...

It's a stupid idea! But not all stupid ideas are wrong, are they?

I should be thinking about Marty. He's the one they're putting into the ground today. He was a decent fellow and deserves attention. I remember saying – to Malcolm, I think – that I'd rather show up at that birthday party than just appear at his funeral. And I remember how pleased I'd been by Ronnie's report that Marty wouldn't mind if I came. Or, anyway, that's what Ronnie said that Marty had said. And sometimes, when imagination flags, Ronnie can be telling the truth. (Was it Oscar Wilde who said that? Of whom?)

I still wonder whether I shouldn't have just gone with Ronnie. But I figured I ought to check with Malcolm and Jason, just to make sure they didn't mind, as of course they did. They were both very firm in their disapproval.

So I didn't go. But I am still grateful and pleased about Marty's permission. And that last conversation we had on the telephone, which I take as evidence that he really did want me to come to the party. Or at least wouldn't have minded.

When you hit your tenth decade, you develop a sense of proportion, perhaps. I have something to look forward to, if I can hold out that long.

So I am showing up now, even though I was asked not to come to the funeral itself, so as not to upset Nina in her bereavement. Which is not, apparently, overwhelming enough to allow her to forget her anger at me.

I used to find it flattering, that someone could hold on to such hatred for so long, but by now, I think, it's mostly habit.

But it wasn't worth an argument. Did I really want to listen to a eulogy from some rabbi who didn't even know him? Was I all that keen on reciting once again the prayers in which I am not sure I believe and from which I take so little comfort? What I really wanted was just to be there, and the *there* isn't a funeral home but the actual graveside.

Malcolm's report that his mother had no objection to my being there was a surprise. Even a mystery.

Was Nina being generous? Or were Malcolm and Jason taking a stand and arguing on my behalf?

"Don't go there, boss," says Coward.

As long as Ronnie is there, I won't be the most despised person in the group. Still, even though Ronnie is an outcast, he's their outcast. I'm not theirs anymore. I'm connected only through Jason and Malcolm, am an outsider now, an intrusion. It's possible that no one except Jason and Malcolm will speak to me ... But is that such a bad thing?

To be shunned, as if one were invisible, is an interesting condition, even dramatic. It could be as if I were a ghost they saw but did not want to acknowledge. And in my ghostliness, I would be closer to Marty than any of them.

"And now," the loudspeaker announces, "the Invisible Skaters present ... 'The Face of God!'" And the electric organ booms out with "Amazing Grace," as the many-colored lights play over the ice, on which no one is performing in an intricate choreography of Axels, Camels, spirals, Lutzes, loops, and Salchows. The audience doesn't know what to make of what they're seeing, or not seeing, and cannot decide whether to applaud or boo ... But how can they boo for God? So they cheer and stamp their feet.

"Poor taste," du Calme suggests, shaking his head, as if *Goose Bumps* were a perfectly reasonable undertaking.

He knows what I am thinking, of course, but he also knows he can rely on me to argue for him, as of course I do, pointing out that the stresses of life in Guatemala, El Salvador, Colombia, and Peru are such that *Goose Bumps* is relatively tame. Where he draws the line is snuff ice capades, in which someone is actually killed. He will have no part of that kind of show, not for all the colons, balboas, sols, and pesos in the world. He has – would you believe? – principles! He also has "just a touch of malaria" and jaundice, which he picked up, he thinks, at the Devil's Island Holiday Inn and Casino, where people politely assumed he was part Chinese.

"Not that I criticize those who do such things," he tells me, demonstrating that he is basically a liberal, permissive, and therefore decent fellow. "It's just that I'm not comfortable, myself."

It's as if he were apologizing for some irrational quirk.

"After all, the entertainment industry is a service business," he says. "Either we give the public what it wants or we perish, ourselves."

Where are these people coming from, I ask myself, as if I had no idea. (For my own irrational quirks, I fear that no apology is possible.)

My prejudice, for instance, against figure skating in general and ice shows in particular, may not be a quirk, but it is certainly a minority position. Those kitschy costumes and that terrible music ... What kind of sport is performed to music? Well, the women's floor exercises in gymnastics, and synchronized swimming, but they have that same touch of vulgarity to them. And, alas, the NFL has decided that even football needs jazzing up, so that their half-time highlights come with signature music that the real games now seem to lack. Figure skating, being neither an athletic event nor an art form, tries to combine both these domains and inevitably betrays them both. Then, the champions of amateur competitions look to cash in on a vulgarization and commercialization of what was already vulgar to begin with in those anomalous displays that are beyond satire.

Du calme, du calme, says du Calme, adjusting the unlit cigar he keeps clenched in his teeth as if it were some Freudian badge of office. You have more pressing worries at the moment, n'est-ce pas?

I do not answer, hoping that perhaps he will go away.

What also shuts me up is my sense that he is correct. With a sinking feeling, I realize that there is nothing I can say to refute him.

There are another couple of burnt-out cars, but I do not react much. I am inured. (And is that progress?)

The route is ugly but efficient, and it appears that I am likely to get there almost half an hour ahead of time. I'll be there before the hearse and the funeral procession with all their headlights lit, which is a custom that originates, I suppose, with military caravans, but in civilian life has come to signify mourning, if not actual grief. No one has exploited the possibilities of gradation that the control panel offers – high beams for deepest bereavement, or parking lights for a modest show of sympathy for another's loss. One would not want to go so far as to attempt to simulate actual weeping with the windshield spray and the wipers, and wailing, with the horns, but the gradation of the headlights is not such a bad idea.

For those who are utterly undone by a sudden loss, undertakers could provide on some of their limousines a set of lights like those of the state police with the whirling display overhead of red and blue, and a strobe effect from the headlights ...

Too showy? But there could be a market for it anyway.

To whom could one propose such an idea? A letter to the *Times*? Or perhaps to *The Mortician's Monthly*? (Actually, it's called *The Director* and is the official publication of The National Funeral Directors Association, which doesn't have any apostrophe, although it probably should.) A funeral director with the right temperament, either sufficiently officious or just with a certain odd sense of fun, might enjoy giving out these instructions, just to see if he could get the mourners, preoccupied as most of them must be at such a time, to comply with his bizarre instructions.

I must clear my mind of these ravings. For Marty's sake. Although Marty isn't likely to mind. And it strikes me that Ronnie, for all his faults, might be diverted in this difficult time – by which I don't mean only the death of his father but his having to appear this way and suffer the family's disapproval and, even worse, their momentary indulgence ...

If there is a moment that permits, I might tell him this idea. Even though it will look like the two pariahs have sought each other out.

Tant pis, as the Frenchman said, whose aunt went off to micturate. Let them think whatever they want.

❖

An exit sign announces the route number for which I have been looking. Land ho!

The Chinese entrant in the figure-skating competition? No, no. Go away.

He does, and I am grateful to him. And hope that he won't come back, the way the departed tend to do – which is why Jews put those little stones on grave markers, both to indicate that there was someone there making a visit, but also to weigh down the restless ghosts and prevent them from rising up to loom over us like Chagall figures, and perhaps play for us on their blue violins and pester us however they can.

Sometimes they can say comforting things, reminding us that they care about us and wish us well. Or they may merely greet us and make trivial remarks that help pass the timelessness. But more often than not, they will express their disappointment in us, as they did in life, letting us know that we have one way or another failed yet again to live up to their perfectly reasonable expectations. They are impossible to argue with because they know our failings and doubts as well as we do and can address them with surgical accuracy precisely because they are, at least in part, our figments.

Marty may not be playing the violin, but he'll have a tango combo with him and he'll be wearing black tie and patent-leather dancing shoes. And in the shadows behind him, unless I am much mistaken, one of the musicians looks like my father. It can't be, of course, but in these fantasies and nightmares there is nothing that one can reliably exclude. He is playing that accordion-like instrument, the name of which escapes me – the bandoneon? – and he accompanies the dancing, or, say, enables it. He looks very sad, and while that is how performers of tango music often look, it is right for him, exactly the expression I remember, with the corners of his mouth turned down as if his mustache ends were weighing upon him with the griefs of the world.

The burden he carried was his anger and chagrin about Alice, whose transgressions, compared with those of Ronnie, for example, were insignificant. But then my father had invested more of himself in us and his dreams of how we were to live and what we were to become than Marty ever thought of doing. Marty was right, of course, because love, when it reaches a certain pitch, can be dangerous, distorting and smothering.

What she did was to get married, which is what daughters do. It wasn't the marriage, though, but the wedding itself and what happened to our parents' plans and preparations that he couldn't tolerate.

"Mistah Kurtz, he dead," the manager's boy announces in *Heart of Darkness*, but Mr. Kurtz, Alice's fiancé's father, didn't die. He'd had a heart attack, but was out of danger, had been released from the hospital and was home, recuperating. But the Kurtzes couldn't possibly attend the wedding my parents had arranged. The wedding or the dinner party afterwards. And that was perfectly reasonable.

My parents' suggestion – which seems sensible to me, even now – was that Alice and Harvey could marry, could come to the dinner, could leave perhaps at a slightly earlier hour than the original schedule called for, and could go into New York where, in Kurtz's bedroom, they could repeat the ceremony, re-enacting it for his benefit. After all, the invitations had already gone out. The presents had started to appear. The money, a not inconsiderable amount of it, had been paid to the hotel's banquet department and at this late date would not be returned.

But even to mention the money, which I'm sure my father did, would be to falsify the situation. He could talk about the money because to do so was less shameful than to admit his personal humiliation, his dismay at having to notify all the guests – sixty? seventy? a hundred? – that the event had been canceled. What the Kurtzes proposed was that the large wedding should simply be canceled and that Alice and Harvey should be married in their living room where the family could share a bottle of champagne, and that would be that.

No? No! Not right. Not fair. Absolutely unacceptable. For Alice even to relay the proposal of such a thing was a demonstration of her lack of respect and loyalty. How could she contemplate her own parents' humiliation in this way? How could she have listened to such a bizarre idea without making the objections that should have come immediately to mind? How did she expect her parents to feel when she conveyed the Kurtzes' selfish and arrogant suggestion to them? It was, my father said, a manifestation of thoughtlessness and ingratitude so inconceivable and unforgivable that it meant the end of the relationship. No daughter of his could behave in such a way.

I wonder which came first, the emotional truth of the statement or its oratorical formulation? Might it be that the threat, having once been uttered, was then impossible to withdraw? The estrangement that followed turned out to be a drastic and expensive response. It embittered my father's life and, I believe, shortened it considerably.

I can't imagine my parents agreeing to what the Kurtzes wanted, but my father's anger might have spent itself in a matter of months, and there could have been an occasion at which at least there might have been some détente, some rapprochement. The birth of Alice's first child, perhaps? But the words had been said and their iron logic had no give in it anywhere. No daughter of his could behave in this way. She had behaved in this way. Therefore, she was no daughter of his. Q.E.D.

QE 2.

Or RMS Titanic.

From time to time, I have wondered what Alice might have been thinking. Or feeling. Or in some murky way experiencing. I can't persuade myself that it was a grand passion, a *folie amoureuse* that blinded her temporarily but absolutely to what others might think or say. Harvey Kurtz was not the kind of person to inspire any such torrent of irresistible emotion. But the Kurtzes may have bedazzled her. My guess would be that it was Sonia more than Joel, for she was the manipulative one, demanding and formidable, as Joel never was, even when healthy.

She was also the one with the money, and there was, I understand, quite a lot of that. Enough, anyway, so that Joel had pretty much retired from the practice of law and for years had been devoting himself full time to looking after his wife's investments. Such a career choice is seldom without psychological consequences. But I can only surmise – and I met them only once, and that was many years ago.

So their presence in my mind is much like that of Kurtz in Marlow's mind, a vague looming from the heart of darkness, a menace upriver that has few details but must have held for Alice a certain glamour. There were no heads on poles, but... there were the artichokes. And the cruelty the Kurtzes showed Alice the first time Harvey brought her home for dinner.

Artichokes were on offer, cold, with a vinaigrette. There is nothing remarkable about that and nothing menacing, unless of course the guest has never before seen an artichoke. We were not deprived, financially or socially, but ... artichokes weren't what we'd ever been served.

I don't remember my own first encounter with that peculiar vegetable, a relative, I believe, of the thistle, but whenever it was, and under whatever circumstances, my initiation carried with it no emotional trauma. Alice was less lucky. What she did that evening in the Kurtzes' dining room, not knowing any better, was to pick up her knife and fork ... .

Sonia, at that moment, could perfectly well have pulled a leaf off her own artichoke and dipped it into the vinaigrette, and seeing this Alice would have taken the hint, put down her silverware, and followed her hostess's example. That would have been the decent way to treat a young guest, I think. But Sonia had a streak of cruelty in her, and perhaps also a mother's possessiveness that disposed her to be less than kind to this girl who had come into her life and now threatened to displace her in her son's affections. For whatever reason, she stopped and watched – they all watched – as Alice attacked the artichoke with knife and fork.

I was not there, but it is easy enough to imagine the critical thirty seconds or so of silence, after which Alice must have realized that they were all staring at her, and then, suddenly, rudely, laughing aloud.

A wretched business, but a wound like that, when it heals, can leave adhesions. Or, to put it another way, Alice would have seen a way out of her humiliation by identifying with the Kurtzes and, particularly, with Sonia and her grande-dame pretensions. The alternative would have been for Alice to admit that she had been made to feel foolish and inadequate by the frivolous cruelty of a rich, trivial woman to whose spoiled son she was now engaged.

Had she been able to do that, she could have got up from the table, left the room and the apartment, broken off the engagement, and had a different and almost certainly a better life.

If Alice "betrayed" our parents, it was not when she agreed to the Kurzes' demands about the wedding; it was back then, on that evening in that dining room, when she pretended to join in the laughter that was, after all, directed at her, and at us, and accepted Sonia's instructions about pulling one of the outer leaves off the artichoke, dipping it in the dressing, and pulling it through her nearly closed teeth to get the flesh off the tougher outer membrane.

Our father was a proud man. Alice ought to have learned from him how to maintain her pride and, when that was impossible, how to walk away from whatever it is that offers an intolerable affront.

I remember thinking and, somewhere earlier in these pages, writing that it would be interesting to do a novel about a man who chooses to wear a red rather than a blue tie, or, more precisely, the unimaginable consequences of such a small, discrete act. What if Sonia Kurtz had decided to serve shrimp cocktails or pickled herring, rather than the artichokes? Might our lives have been radically different?

Might Alice not have performed those psychic gymnastics that blinded her to the meanness and selfishness du côté de chez Kurtz? Might she have noticed Harvey's self-absorption, Joel's sly, passive-aggressive ruthlessness, and Sonia's viciousness? Her estrangement from her father, the four unpleasant years of her marriage, the acrimony and spitefulness of her divorce might all have been avoided.

And all those years of our father's brokenheartedness.

Or pâté? Pâté is good.

Even, for God's sake, salmon mousse …

4

There they come, the cortège with the hearse in the lead and then the train of cars with their headlights on. No flatbed trucks with those high-powered searchlights that grace openings of movies and sales at used-car lots. Nothing excessive or showy. Not even that strolling combo with the two guitars and the marimba and the bandoneon that I have somehow come to associate with Marty's obsequies.

Nina would be annoyed to know that I've allowed such a thought to cross my mind, and there would be no point in attempting to explain to her that there is nothing disrespectful in it. It is a conversation we don't have to go through, which is a small blessing for which I'd be more thankful if I were more confident that there aren't worse pitfalls awaiting me. I am worried, not so much for my own sake or even for Marty's as for the boys', that I'll say something quite unintentionally that will provoke Nina and elicit that nastiness of which she always seems capable. A graveside tirade in which Nina, out of control, hurls imprecations at my head, and maybe a few of those rocks that mourners have left conveniently on nearby headstones. That she is mourning her father's death makes such an eruption more likely rather than less. Suffering, or even mild discomfort, generally brings out the worst in people.

I try to summon up some sympathy for her at the loss of her parent, but he was in his nineties and he'd had a long and generally fortunate life. He can hardly be said to have been cut down in the first flower of his youth. And his last few months were not easy. Pain-free, mostly, but there wasn't much for him to enjoy or to look forward to with any eagerness.

Happiness is when it's good and looks to be getting even better. We are proud of our prefrontal lobes and our sense of time, but they do get in the way of our having a good time. I remember a cartoon, maybe by Peter Arno, in which one débauché in an erotic crowd scene is asking a nude playmate, "What are you doing after the orgy?"

After ninety-odd years, Marty must have had the habit of living in time, but toward the end, this would have become, I suspect, increasingly burdensome.

The grief, then, of his survivors is mostly for ourselves, because he was a decent fellow and we'll miss him.

I am aware that I am taking a moment to consult my feelings this way because, once Nina has appeared, I will no longer be fully in control but will mostly be reacting to whatever she says and does. If she is excessive and self-indulgent, as I expect her to be, then I will balk and, while I hope I won't say anything or show anything, a part of me will have become embattled. It could then be all but im-

possible for me to feel even an appropriate sadness for
Marty's death.

It is a subdued March day, clear but overcast, and not
too warm but with a freshness in the air that at least hints
at the possibility of spring's arrival. The hours just before
dawn are those in which people tend to die, as if they had
been trying to hold out through the night to another allot-
ment of light. Either they despair in those hours before
dawn or, as I fear, they sense somehow that pre-dawn
relenting of the darkness and relax just a little, and it's that
relaxation that undoes them. An early robin sounding its
notes, and…

But Marty was in Florida.

It's my father I'm thinking about.

Again.

When our father died, Alice wept bitter tears, as she ought
to have done. It wasn't that she missed him more than
anyone else did, but now there couldn't even be a dream
of reconciliation, of some apology and forgiveness that each
of them must have thought about at odd moments.

I had supposed, when Harvey left her, that there might
be an opportunity. She was now abandoned and betrayed,
and all those operatic fantasies my father must have entertained had now been fulfilled.

Of course, I have no way of knowing what fantasies
he might have… What did I say? Entertained? No, they'd
have been a torment. And I am only imagining what, in his
place, I might have been thinking. The truth, however, is
often worse than our idle imaginings. And the worst case
is that he wished her well, that he blamed Joel and Sonia
Kurtz, or, even worse than that, blamed himself somehow,

for having done something wrong. She was his daughter, after all, and he loved her. And to spare her the onus of responsibility, he might very well have tried to shoulder it himself, so as to find some way of taking upon himself the responsibility for her terrible decision about the wedding. Had he been the one to have turned her callous and thoughtless? Had it been some failure on his part that the gods were punishing, and were they the ones who were using her and the Kurtzes, too, as their almost innocent instruments?

No, of course not. But the alternative was for him to blame Alice, and to admit, therefore, that his love for her was not and never had been reciprocated. And which of us is hard enough to allow even for a moment such a thought about one of our own children?

Our father died not at the coming of spring but at the winter solstice, the darkest and longest night of the year. It was where he had learned to live. It was home. And having reached that comfortable and familiar nadir, he could expire.

They get out of the cars. There isn't a verb for that, is there? One can debark or, as they now say with a back formation, deplane, but one can't decar. They do, however, emerge from their vehicles, and the greetings are uneventful. Malcolm and Jason welcome me with what seems an appropriate show of pleasure, given the venue. Nina acknowledges me with a slight nod that might have been calculated by a Japanese protocol expert. Her husband, Allen, is affable and he shakes my hand. Ronald comes walking up, having presumably parked some distance away. He is smiling, almost cheerful, but that could be the effect of the Italian sunglasses. For a son at his father's graveside, he seems to be doing well. Unless, of course, this is put on, a mask for what he not unreasonably takes to be a hostile audience.

I wonder if Marty's death means that he'll be getting some money, which, presumably, he needs. Or will the sums he's already received now be deducted from his share of the estate? Will there be anything left?

I wonder, too, about the coincidence of his homosexuality and dishonesty, so that one is fearful about criticizing him for his financial irregularities lest one appear to be a gay-bashing bigot. It's a kind of moral ju-jitsu he'd find more amusing if he didn't have to rely on it so heavily and so often.

There is a young rabbi I have never seen before and whom I'd be willing to bet Marty never saw either. And there are the funeral home functionaries, in their black suits and black ties, efficiently negotiating the transfer of the coffin from the hearse to the collapsible chrome trolley that will take it the last ten yards or so up the aisle to the gravesite, where I can see an array of folding chairs and, over the mound of earth displaced by the back-hoe, a mat of artificial grass of an implausibly bright green that is supposed to spare us the depressing sight of actual dirt, which reminds us of what Donne called "this posthume death, this death after death, nay, this death after burial, this dissolution after dissolution, this death of corruption and putrefaction, of vermiculation and incineration, of dissolution and dispersion in and from the grave."

He does hit you over the head with it, doesn't he? The vividness of it is awesome, and of course awe on the part of the congregation was exactly what the sermon was aiming for.

Vermiculation, indeed!

The rabbi will be less vivid. For him it's another gig. The fact that he never knew Marty must make it a comfortable transaction, a generalized contemplation of death which is subversively pleasant when it happens to someone we don't know. The fresh air on our own faces seems all the sweeter in the presence of this memento mori. A few prayers, an envelope with a check in it, and then a nice lunch. What better day can one imagine? The odd thing is that I can't imagine Marty's spirit making any objection, even if it could. He was a realist.

As my father was not.

The party makes its way toward the gravesite, treading without compunction over the graves of others ... I follow along at the tail end of the not very numerous group and, as we walk, I notice some of the names on the stones: Fogelman, Mittleman, and Kuperman are planted almost cheek by jowl, in one of those coincidences that both invites and defies novelists.

They don't mind, being dead. They can lie quietly, untroubled by a propinquity that seems to be the setup for a joke without a punch line.

But there is a punch line, which I remember. The names weren't quite these, but were close enough. There was a long dark corridor on the third floor of the building where my father had his office, and on the way to the men's room at the end of that hallway, you passed a series of names like these: Fogelman, Mittleman, Kuperman. And then Gentlemen.

It was my father's joke, and for it to return to me now is a gift. Even though I can see how the cues in the external world prompted those neurons to fire, it still feels as though, in this cemetery, my father's ghost has contrived to greet me, to speak, as it sometimes seems able to do. And which of us is so heartless as to deny the possibility?

For reasons that I cannot understand, they are going to say a few words. Nina and Allen, and Nina's Uncle Jack, who was Marty's younger brother. And Malcolm and Jason. And Ronnie? (Which is worse? For him to speak or to have to remain silent? Whichever is worse is what will surely occur.)

Oughtn't this all to have happened back at the funeral home? Having been excluded from those ceremonies, I had hoped to be spared their assault on my sensibilities. But no such luck. I will nevertheless have to listen to maudlin and mawkish pronouncements about a man I liked, or, more likely, I will have to exert myself to not listen, to divert my skittish attention by screaming that silent scream that Rabbi Nachman of Bratslav recommends, and dancing his small and invisible dance.

Or, more likely, I will have to allow Timmy and Donna to do the number Coward brought them out here to perform for Kuperman, Fogelman, and Mittleman sitting at the judges' table in their shiny serge suits. And there will be music, of course, by Peppy Paco and his Perky Peronistas, who will plink away with marimba and bandoneon in an up-tempo version of the Kaddish, to which the sequined skaters will do their program of leaps and spins.

What would be even worse would be to listen to Nina and Allen and Uncle Jack talk about Marty's wonderful qualities, which most of us were perfectly well aware of during his lifetime. (For whom do they suppose themselves to be performing?)

But would that be worse? I don't know anymore. I don't know anything. I used to take a certain pride in be-

ing able to flee into these mental forests where the twit-
terings and roars of bizarre creatures could distract me from
whatever was too sordid or tedious to abide in what
unimaginative people call the real world. But I've been
upcountry for too long, and I'm tired of the nonsense. My
head aches from the racket. I am oppressed by these
flickerings and scurryings and, worse, dismayed by my
inability to control them.

Or, more clearly, my inability to control myself. People
who are not in control are lunatics, maniacs, idiots, socio-
paths …

"Du calme, du calme," says du Calme, but he has not
been there, has not seen in the light of smoky torches those
ghastly heads stuck up on poles, has not dined at the
Kurtzes' table with the naked natives dancing and laughing as the missionaries attempt to eat artichokes with their
ivory-handled knives and forks.

I want them all to go away and leave me alone. I want
to be like a normal person. (But are there normal people?)
I want there to be nothing but white noise, a gentle sound
of surf punctuated only by the intermittent rustle of palm
trees in a sea breeze, and the almost palpable weight of
sunlight on my closed eyelids.

No, no, I am not turning sappy. This is therapeutic, believe
it or not. This is an induction technique, and one can lower
one's blood pressure and heart rate by thinking of such
desirable locations and pleasant conditions. Concentrate on
breathing and think of the surf and the palm trees … . Or
a flowery meadow, if you'd rather, except that if you suffer from hay fever, that idea may make you start to sneeze.
The metaphors that poets and novelists have taken for

granted for years, therapists have put to work for the benefit of their patients.

It's sad in a way, like a racehorse pulling a milk wagon or a team of poodles harnessed to a dogsled. Utility, which once knew its place and tugged its forelock, now runs the manor, while the duke puts in long, strenuous days greeting the tourists, examining the books of the gift shop, and doing whatever other menial chores are required in his almost hopeless effort to pay off the death duties ...

No, never mind the duke, who is making me grind my teeth in displaced rage. Let us rather go back to the beach. The sun on the son-of-a-bitching beach!

I am not involved. It makes no never-mind to me. Nothing Nina or any of the others can say will make any more difference to me than it can to Marty. I must learn from him that wonderful inertness, that earthen patience he is discovering, that he will perfect as he learns from his neighbors, Kuperman, Fogelman, and Mittleman. In a clubby way, they will pursue together the perfect relaxation of vermiculation, that ultimate meditative exercise.

The trumpet of resurrection, if it comes, will bring with it a certain regret from those who have excelled in the achievement of that exquisite indifference I am imagining.

"No trumpets," Marty used to say at the bridge table.

It wasn't much of a joke, but I welcomed it because it showed that even that hardheaded man of business was not immune to what I had thought was my own peculiar foible.

If only a few people are like this, it's a disease. If everyone is like this, then it's the human condition.

Which is also, perhaps, a disease, but not one that's likely to be covered by your usual health plan. It would be considered, at least theologically, a pre-existing condition.

❖

The rabbi is reading from Ecclesiastes, a not unprecedented selection, I'm afraid. But I may suppose that his boredom with this inevitable passage is balanced against his fear of puzzling or even offending his audience. As likely as not, we'll get the twenty-third psalm, too. He might have asked the mourners whether they would prefer something else, but what else could they ask for? What else did they know?

So he is reading this bit of wisdom, which is supposed to be comforting, but I am not comforted. Instead, I am puzzled. Are irreligious people soothed by the idea of the faith they don't practice? Or, moving the same paradox into a different domain, are subliterates who do not ordinarily read poetry cheered by the idea that, whether they've been paying attention or not, it's out there and they could, if they chose, avail themselves of it?

Marty was never a big reader. Or religious, so far as I ever was aware of. So whether the rabbi is asserting the truth or the beauty of the passage, he could be said to be indicting poor Marty as much as offering comfort to his spirit and to those who cared enough about him to drive out here to the middle of Long Island to witness his burial.

> A time to be born, and a time to die;
> a time to plant, and a time to pluck up what is
>   planted;
> a time to kill and a time to heal;
> a time to break down and a time to build up;
> a time to weep and a time to laugh;
> a time to mourn, and a time to dance …

Was that it, though? The reference to dancing? If she was consulted, was that what Nina had in mind? Or is it merely a happy accident, something the divine author thought might grace the occasion?

Is it perhaps even Marty himself, waving from the great beyond at this sad-sack rabbi who is just doing his job, or at his son and daughter who are grieving?

These are fanciful questions of which Marty would not ordinarily have approved. On the other hand, the real world, without fancy, is less than itself, an uninteresting abstraction without richness or color.

I find myself looking at Ronnie to see how he's holding up. Well enough, apparently, and appearance is what counts. Or is that merely what I was expecting? Actually, he looks a little shopworn this morning. His shirt is not dazzling. The knot of the tie is just slightly off center. He generally manages to look prosperous and trim, even dapper, either for business reasons or for the sake of his social life, but in this unforgiving daylight the lines around his eyes and mouth seem deeper than I remember them, as if the effort of smiling through adversity had somehow marked the flesh.

Still, a stranger, inspecting us all, would have no reason to pick him out as especially distraught, as my sister was at our father's funeral. Her grief, after all, was mixed with that rage one feels toward those to whom one has behaved badly. At the funeral and at the graveside, she felt obliged to suppress it, but it seeped through like the chemicals in some toxic waste site so that, in her wracked sobs, there was a terrible bitterness.

I could not help wondering, perhaps unkindly, whether our father, if he had been aware of her torment, would have been distressed or pleased.

Love has its ups and downs, but estrangement is a steady state. The negative presence is always there, like…

Like what? Okay, smart guy! Put all this involuntary logorrhea and phanopoeia to work for a change. Find a new metaphor.

… like the note that rings in the head of someone with tinnitus. Bedrich Smetana was afflicted in this way, I think. Locked away in a nuthouse with an E-flat or whatever it was sounding in his head. Continually? Continuously?

All the time.

He could still write music, but he never allowed himself that particular note, which would have been tantamount to giving in to his affliction.

For Alice, the estrangement would have been less oppressive during our father's lifetime. He was the one who refused to see her or even to talk to her on the telephone. She could tell herself that even if she had been wrong about the wedding, he was wrong too, and more seriously wrong, because she had made an effort and he was the one who had refused to see her, so that it was now his doing. And she could always hope that, one day, there might come some relenting. But after his death, that hope was gone. Dead and defunct. What is death but another estrangement?

And similarly, for Ronnie, his hopes – he must have entertained some notion, however, implausible, of a reformation and reconciliation – are also dead.

Tantamount is the name of the horse your aunt rode in on.

The best I can hope, for Ronnie's sake, is that his grief is powerful enough to blot out, at least for the moment, all other thought. In moments of real agony, we are excused from self-awareness. Or, to put it another way, the pain eclipses any sense of self, or even becomes the self. One is nothing more than the throb or keening …

It is not a metaphor. I hear a keening, but it is not from the vocal cords or the nervous system of any of us here at the graveside. It is a wailing siren in the distance, out in the world of the living, some ambulance, fire engine, or police cruiser on the job. Or a showier cortège?

No, this is real. As Ronnie's pain must be real. And if it absorbs him sufficiently, then he doesn't give a damn what any of the rest of us are thinking. As I may allow myself to imagine, he is hardly aware of us. He and his father and the hole in the ground are real. And perhaps that siren has entered into the field of his consciousness because its wail conveniently represents the sound he can just barely keep himself from making but which the world has contrived to supply.

The sound is curiously comforting, even though we know that it represents someone in acute distress. Misery may not particularly love company, but it can be comforting to know that one is not the only victim and that stochastic catastrophes bestrew the landscape. What is remarkable is that our prosperity and good fortune have lasted as long as they have without some sudden reversal.

Am I being too fanciful here? Probably so, for Ronnie seems altogether oblivious. In which case, he is closer to Marty than any of those who are listening to the rabbi or thinking about what they will say when it comes time to deliver their remarks. Almost certainly, he is closer to Marty than I am, or at least in his numb sorrow less afflicted by this inner yammer that diminishes everything I experience to the dimensions of a Punch and Judy show.

Of course, the reason that Punch and Judy shows have survived for so long is that they embody a brusque truth about our lives we could not otherwise comfortably admit. (Even so, which of us would want to join those packs of grotesque puppets and make their diminutive commedia dell'arte stages our home?)

Even in those moments when the buffoonery relents, the quality of my attention is tainted, as if it were one of those stages from which the puppets have just departed or onto which they are about to make an entrance. Its space is blemished.

Le style, c'est l'homme. Or is it his sickness?

Or do those propositions turn out to affirm the same thing?

My stomach grumbles, inaudibly I hope. But it is enough to remind me that I have not had breakfast. Just coffee in the car. And that we are captives of a comical organism, an unwieldy and unreliable physiological apparatus that we laugh at as children and then, as we grow older and more sophisticated, we learn to put up with but are never altogether comfortable about.

Or one could say that these comic turns are the body's way of calling us back to the concerns of this world. The temptation to higher thought is everywhere, and without such promptings we'd be subjected to the endless maunderings of an interminable series of rabbis, telling us what they think we ought to hear, or, on occasions like this, what we want to hear.

"Loving husband, father, grandfather …" is a phrase I pick out of the static. Well, it's not much of a claim, is it? A successful progenitor, whose progeny produced progeny. Are we to be judged as stud horses? (Tantamount, son of Tea-biscuit.) Or is the rabbi suggesting that Marty's having sired issue was in some sense life affirming? It's not necessarily where he was going with his remarks, if indeed they had any particular direction, but it is the kindest construction I can put on this fragment of his remarks. It can't be all demented blather. Nina would have noticed and would have an (even) angrier expression on her face.

So, he was life affirming. And here are the results of his affirmation: Nina and Ronnie, and Jason and Malcolm …

Had Marty been gay, and had Nina never been born, how different my life would have been.

Jason and Malcolm would never have happened, but then, as Sophocles (I think) says, it is better never to have been born.

Is it? I don't know. I don't know.

I just hope they don't think so.

What death offers is an end to the struggle and even a kind of reconciliation. Our parents' plot has two empty spaces, one for me and one that was obviously intended for Alice. I am older than she and male, so the odds are that she will survive me. And the empty grave site will go to her, so that, if she chooses, she can be buried with the three of us. All together again, as in the old days, having a good time …

Not that I remember so many good times. Or, rather, what I remember is fragmentary and improvisational. Trips to that little airfield, for instance, where we'd watch small planes take off and land in what was little more than a pasture with a paved strip and, at one end, a windsock on a pole. But it was up the road that ran by the reservoir and the water surrounded by pine trees was pretty. And across the road from the airfield, there was the Log Cabin, which had a take-out window where you could get hamburgers and hot dogs and Cokes.

The Sunday drive is an almost forgotten ritual now, but we used to do that, go out into the country, and the airfield and the Log Cabin were about the right distance from the house. So we'd go there, and there wasn't any pressure, and it was quiet and comfortable. Even the planes, unless you were right next to them, were like big toys that buzzed more than they roared. They were kites we didn't have to run with to get up in the air, and didn't have to worry about getting caught in tree branches.

I can see it, although what I'm seeing looks more like a faded photograph than what the place must actually have been. Alice is in braids. I am wearing a checked shirt and a windbreaker, and my ears stick out the way they used to do. Mother is wearing a hat. Dad is pointing up at one of the planes. Or just upward, because that's what he did, urging us to achieve and improve ourselves … ?

No, that's unfair. He's pointing at a plane.

It's nothing special, just something we used to do. But that is what makes it special. It is un-posed, and we are, for the moment, happy.

He is younger than I am now, and I want to keep him there at the Log Cabin. I want to protect him from what I know is waiting to happen to him, as if I were the father and he the son. I want to fend off what is waiting to happen to us all. If all these things had never happened, what burdens of blame might be lifted from our frail shoulders – Ronnie's, Alice's, and mine, too, of course.

I am aware that tears are welling up in my eyes and I wipe them away with the heels of my palms.

The tears are not for Marty, although that's what my sons must think. Jason comes over to stand next to me, and he puts his arm around my shoulder to comfort me. I put my arm around his waist in a gesture of acknowledgment and thanks. Whatever Sophocles says, I am glad he's here, if only for selfish reasons.

Even if there were an opportunity to do so, I would not correct his misapprehension about the cause of my emotion. Indeed, I cannot say that his surmise is absolutely wrong.

When love generalizes, it can occasion jealousy; we are, we can afford to be, more generous about grief.

5

Nina is about to hold forth. I do not want to hear her. I want not to hear her. I am content to let Fogelman and Mittelman entertain us with an exhibition of juggling and the twirling of plates on sticks, to be accompanied by Paco and his carioca crew, who will perform their own arrangement of "The Sabre Dance" by Our Man Khatchaturian.

Juggling and plate twirling are therefore, by my previously enunciated rule, not sports. Which is why they are not represented at the Olympics, although, now that I think about it, I don't see why on earth they shouldn't be.

Kuperman and Gentleman will perform tricks on the unicycle, doing a kind of mechanized dance and playing catch with whiffle balls.

In life, they were probably not such cut-ups, but they might well have had the desire buried deep within their psyches. Only now are they allowed to satisfy this long-deferred yearning, not acting it out, because they are incapable of action, but imposing it on innocent passersby like myself, whose minds they can make their arenas.

Mexicans, who understand these things better than we, have fun on the Day of the Dead.

We pull long faces and leave the cavorting to the departed, to whose lively antics we try not to allude.

Trapeze artists are always said to be "death-defying" – but these, being dead already, have nothing to lose and are at best life-defying. One false step and the grinning performers risk having to come back to this world to do it all over again, which is perhaps the menace that the band is suggesting to us with the presto drumbeat and the bright blare of Khatchaturian's relentless trombone glissandi.

They are tireless. Or they have no sense of time, which is, *sub specie aeternitatis*, a difficult concept. They are altogether into it, while my attention is flighty and unreliable. There are, at any rate, lapses, and during one of these I hear Nina saying, "He was a most forgiving man," and then there is a pause, and I look up to see what has happened to her.

She is glaring, first at Ronnie and then at me. We are adduced as the exemplars of Marty's forgiving nature. Adduced and traduced, because clearly, if it had been up to her, he'd not have forgiven either of us. And our presence here is an affront. An affront by which, in this aside, she lets us know she is taken aback.

Oh, for pity's sake. But there is no pity in her. No relenting.

I am an ex-husband, and I find it ever so slightly flattering to be the occasion still of such enmity. But Ronnie has come all the way out here from the city to attend his father's interment, and he might reasonably have expected the kind of truce that combatants observe in the most uncivil civil wars.

Should I smile and wave, acknowledging her notice?

Should I mount Tantamount, my one-trick pony, and follow Kuperman's unicycle around the ring, cavorting with the relentlessly cheery ghosts?

I look up at the mackerel sky as if to ask heaven to bear witness that I've come here to pay my respects. And nothing Nina has to say can change that.

Childish of her. But here she is, Marty's child. An orphan now.

She is perhaps hiding in her anger, for the comfort it gives her. The sorrow of it she will have to learn to sidle up to.

I remember the right retort. What Ronnie and I could say, and it would be surprising and more effective if we did it together, is: "I'm rubber; you're glue. Whatever you say bounces off me and sticks to you."

Being here with Nina is bracing. One's recollection of spite dims over time, but she is able, with just a passing remark, to refresh the enmity that obtains between us. And this makes me think of my parents, and … and what the estrangement must have done to them.

My mother was loyal enough, or submissive enough, not to argue with my father about Alice. But she was also independent enough to venture into the city to see Alice sometimes. No matter what my father might think, she would have been forgiving enough to sneak into town, perhaps claiming to my father that she was going to a matinée, and instead visiting her daughter.

And my father, who wasn't a fool, would have suspected, after a while.

Maybe, at least at first, she actually went to the theater, so that she could buttress her alibi, producing a Playbill and even talking about the performance. But that would have cut precious hours from the time she had with her daughter. So she might have given that up, and "the theater" turned into a code word, the meaning of which was clear enough to both of them.

It would have seemed to my father as though my mother was being unfaithful to him. And he would have moped all the time she was gone, and would have sulked for days afterward.

I hate to imagine this, but its practical aspects are all but irresistible. Did mother telephone Alice? And did my father examine the phone bills? Or did my mother have some sort of arrangement by which Alice called her after some predetermined signal – one ring and a hang-up, and a second time, to confirm. And then Alice, knowing that it was mother and she was alone, could call back …

That was before caller ID, which would have made their lives easier.

But not better.

The need for subterfuge would have made the whole business more sordid and therefore more painful.

❖

What Nina seems to be telling us is that her father was a nice man, a wonderful man. Who will be missed, &c, &c.

Of whom can one not say this?

Joel Kurtz, of course. Who lived longer, with his defective heart, than my father and mother. He outlived Sonia and outlasted Alice's marriage to his son, Harvey. He was the poster boy for those who believe that the good die young. At his interment, there really ought to have been clowns and jugglers, magicians, mimes, and buskers. A block party. A fiesta.

Marty, a decent fellow, was the exception that proves that there's a rule.

And that seems not to be my thought, but Allen's. At some low level, and however reluctantly, I seem to be paying attention. Nina is no longer speaking. Allen, her new husband, is now doing his duty. And he's the one who has made the remark about Marty being the exception that proves the rule – about how the good die young.

Clearly, this had to have been Nina's idea. Allen is telling us – Marty's relatives – what a privilege it was to have known this man.

Why should this be necessary?

That it's what Nina wanted is a sufficient answer.

She got the house. She packed up some of my things and sent them on. And what she didn't pack, she gave away. Or so she said. But some of the stuff she gave to Allen, who showed up at Jason's wedding wearing what I recognized as one of my old sport coats.

A thoughtless lapse?

My guess was that he was unaware of it. He's just
vague enough to have reached into the closet and grabbed
whatever came to hand. But Nina knew. And she would
have considered for a while whether or not to suggest that
he wear something else. And she must have decided that
it would be amusing for her to see my reaction when I
realized that her new husband was wearing her old
husband's jacket, that we were replaceable parts. Inter-
changeable elements were a vital part of the industrial revolution, and they seem to have worked their way into the
social revolution, too.

I reacted by not letting her see any reaction.

I wondered whether he'd had to have it retailored, but
I didn't ask.

"Absolutely right, boss," Coward prompts from the
back seat of my car, where he's been dozing. He rearranges
himself and goes back to his nap.

I could change the bastard's name, I guess. Or kill him
off. It's not such a wonderful joke.

True, maybe, but not funny.

And, anyway, what good would that do? Like
Kuperman and Fogelman, he'd just come back, more vivid
and more annoying than ever.

I could perhaps go back and expunge him, rewriting
to remove all evidence of his ever having been …

It that a Roman curse? Or is it Jewish?

It's what we all fear and what we know is waiting for
us. It's what each of us is thinking about, even if we're not
speaking of it, here at Marty's open grave.

I may not be the only one to have a Coward dozing in
the car.

❖

And Uncle Jack says that he was an honorable man, a man whose word other men of business could rely on.

It's a slightly odd thing to be saying, but, on second thought, maybe not. I'd forgotten about that business, back before Nina and I met: in the boom and bust that followed World War II, Marty expanded the business a little more aggressively than he should have, and it failed. And he went under. But then he paid back every nickel he owed, even though he wasn't legally obligated to do so. It's what every guy thinks he's going to do when he declares bankruptcy. But Marty actually did it. With interest. It took him fifteen years.

"I told him he was crazy to do it," Uncle Jack says. "But he never listened to me. And he was right. And I was wrong. And I never told him that. So I'm saying it now."

See? See what I mean? The whole damned story may be elsewhere. Or to put it more tactfully, there are other stories that are going on simultaneously – like Uncle Jack's, in which I figure as a shadowy presence, just as he is here, a wraith, a momentarily convenient supernumerary who comes to life and all but tears the fabric of these maunderings. But in the name of truth, that must be admitted. Truth is important in fiction. Or is it only the appearance of truth we want, the odd funky aroma, that intimate musky tang?

6

What can Malcolm and Jason say?

It is an uncomfortable question, I realize, especially after Nina's performance. That he was, as she said, "forgiving" can be turned around so as to constitute an indictment of Ronnie and me. Or at least it reminds everyone that we were and are in need of forgiveness. That he was, as the fuzzy locution puts it, "always there for us," can also be refracted so as to cast an unflattering light on me, because I left, or was thrown out, or whatever you choose to believe after a series of events so muddled I have no accurate one-word description. No-fault divorces have plenty of fault to be shared around in roughly equal measure. In any event, I wasn't "always there" for them.

I am being tetchy, perhaps? It's something I learned from my father, and while I try not to let the slights of others eat my guts out, I can't help thinking that, however ruinously expensive his behavior was, it was also principled and, in a certain sense, "right." And that stomach rumble I experienced might have been its anticipatory signal, its way of letting me know that it was ready for whatever is about to be put on my plate for me to digest.

These metaphors do have their dark side.

Not that Malcolm and Jason are fools. They are both cagey enough to understand that their mother is not incapable of exploiting even an occasion like this as a chance for a dig at me.

Children of divorce learn shrewdness and circumspection. They are less innocent, less trusting than they'd otherwise have been. It's an advantage in the world, I expect (although, so far as I know, no one has gone so far as to recommend that parents divorce for the sake of their children's education).

I am being nutty? Yes, of course, but in the presence of a nut, not to be nutty is to be nutty. We have here an example of what political scientists call "the rationality of irrationality," which is Herman Kahn's wacko idea and was a part of Nixon's strategic planning in Vietnam. Or you could make a case that most wars are based on some version or other of that bizarre theory. If the outcome of a war is determined by getting one of the combatants to quit, then the more fanatic one is, the better his chances.

The North Vietnamese, the Rwandans, the Kosovars, the Cambodians are not maniacs but philosophers. Or they are maniacs and philosophers. Mania, in this generation, has become a philosophy.

Also depression, but that's another school.

What Malcolm says is that there is a great deal to feel and even to think, but not very much that needs to be said, because all of us here knew Marty and loved him, and were blessed by his presence.

This is true. And also tactful, because it includes me. And is kind to Ronnie. It is unspiteful, which is how Marty was. And how Malcolm is.

He is demonstrating that mansuetude I admired in Marty. He is being kind to me, and also to his mother, walking the fine line that he has learned to negotiate, as if he were one of the acrobats in Kuperman's impromptu troupe.

All Jason says is that Malcolm spoke for both of them, and for all of us. And that, to a considerable degree, Marty is still speaking through them, because he is a part of them and always will be.

And then the Kaddish. And then the ritual shovelfuls of dirt that resound on the casket lid, the first step in Marty's vermiculation and dissolution and dispersion.

Good-bye, Marty.

It's done. I turn away, feeling sad but also justified. I've seen what I came to see and heard those clods of earth hitting the wooden lid of his box.

Should I say something to Nina?

What's to say? That she was, even here, outrageous? Let it go.

Malcolm and Jason are going back with their mother, of course, but they come to hug me and be hugged.

I don't say anything to them, either. I don't have to.

I start back across the other graves toward the roadway where our cars are parked, but someone is calling me. I turn around. It's Ronnie.

"Are you driving?" he asks. "Can you give me a lift?"

"Where to?"

"Any subway station."

"Sure," I say, and on the way to the car I ask him, "You came out with the rest of them, didn't you?"

I'm wondering what happened, how they made him feel so uncomfortable that he didn't want to ride back to town with any of them.

He's not answering. Or, yes, he is, but only with a shake of his head.

Nina didn't let him come to the funeral either. His own father's funeral, and they kept him away.

It crosses my mind that they might have kept him away from the interment, too, except that Nina had made an exception for me, and then must have figured that it'd be nice to lump the two of us together, so that each of us knew in what contempt she held us both.

A matched pair, like Mansuetude and Desuetude.

Together, we are not just pariahs but members of an untouchable caste.

When we get into the car, he tells me, in a calm and reasonable voice, as if he were describing some news event, that he took a bus out and then walked about two miles to get here. And he'd waited for them to show up.

Jesus! It must have taken him … two hours? Three?

"A tough woman," I tell him.

"Oh, yeah."

"I'm sorry about your father," I tell him.

"I know," he says. "Thanks."

I reach out and touch his shoulder. It's not something I often do. But how else can untouchables comfort one another?

7

For the first few minutes, I don't say anything because I don't wish to seem to pry. He doesn't say anything either, and, for a while, it is an innocuous silence, but its quality changes, so that, after a while, it has established itself. To break it would be to violate a kind of decorum that we seem inadvertently to have agreed on. But we can't drive all the way back through Queens without speaking.

"You're looking good," I tell him, not meaning anything by it. It's something one says, after all.

"No, I look like shit."

I glance over and, indeed, he does look less than his usual dapper self. But his father has just died. And he's just taken God knows how many buses and walked how many blocks through the outback of this endless borough to get to the cemetery.

Or did he actually take a cab? Of course, that's what he had to have done. But I'd have seen a cab pull up.

Unless he took a cab, got out, hid somewhere or just sat on one of the benches, waiting for the hearse and the funeral cars to appear. But then why didn't he come out when I showed up?

None of these are questions I can ask him.

And his shirt is less than fresh. And the collar is wilted. Which means either that it isn't its first day or he did walk some distance from the closest bus stop to the cemetery entrance.

"It's not a fashion shoot," I tell him.

"Life is a fashion shoot," he answers. "It's sure as hell not a fountain."

He flashes a quick grin, and then reverts to what I recognize, what doctors would call depression and philosophers would call despair. He looks out the window, which is to say away from me. I let him be, which is the only kindness I can think of.

There are other kindnesses, too. I could ask if he needs money. People who aren't flat broke usually take taxis at a time like this.

But for me to give him anything would be to risk offending Nina. And how much would be enough? Is there, for Ronnie, any such thing as enough?

"How about if I take you into Manhattan?" I offer as a compromise.

"It's out of your way, isn't it?"

"It's one way to go. I'd actually save a few dollars, the way the tolls are set up."

"That'd be fine," he says. "Thanks." And he looks out at the scenery, as if there were something fascinating about these red brick apartment houses and used car lots that we're passing.

The silence reasserts itself so that I am left with my own thoughts about him, even while he's sitting next to me.

Most of the time, when I think of him, which isn't very often, it is with a certain disdain. Not because he's gay or even because he's an embezzler and a petty crook (as I've said, I don't know the details), but because he's a victim of his own fantasies. His grasp of reality is uncertain, which is how he gets into trouble. And he becomes, himself, diaphanous and almost ectoplasmic, so that one can't take him seriously.

His victims, I'm sure, take him seriously, but only in the way that those who suffer from a disease take their bacterium or virus, admitting that they have been affected by these nearly weightless beings. Morally, they are altogether without substance. As Ronnie is, too, I think. He's just not all there.

Marty knew this, and it probably saddened him. But it didn't kill him.

If my father could have thought about Alice in such a way, he might have saved himself a lot of grief.

We're approaching the Midtown Tunnel. From the back seat, Coward tells me there were probably better ways to go.

I pay him no mind. The thing is that we've managed it and will get to Manhattan. In the tunnel's relative darkness, Ronnie allows himself to say what he's been thinking. "It's not as if it was unexpected or anything, and you think you're prepared for it, but it still gets to you."

Nina's spite? Or Marty's death? Or both?

"Yes," I say, "it does," because either way I can agree.

And then there is the daylight and the exit, and a couple of blocks later we're stopped for a red light and Ronnie says, "I'll get out here, then. Thanks." And then, after a beat, "Thanks for everything."

"It sounds too formal, but ... my condolences."

He gets out of the car and walks away in the opposite direction from the traffic.

I turn and watch him disappear among the pedestrians.

Nina has her reasons for excluding him. As my father had his reasons for cutting Alice off that way.

As I have reasons for not talking to Alice. But would I want her to hurt the way Ronnie is apparently hurting?

Or am I just trying to protect myself?

For my father and Nina to be joined together that way on the same side of the question is not at all comfortable for me.

But they are not the same. My father wasn't trying to hurt Alice or make her feel bad. He wanted only to protect himself, to pull back from the source of the pain. Nina's vindictiveness wasn't in him, although Alice would have been hard put to see the difference.

I don't think I'm being spiteful either. It's just that it is too depressing to keep up the pretense that we are behaving like brother and sister and all is in order, when, at any moment, she is able to demonstrate the contrary. If I don't expect anything of her, she can't disappoint me.

Like my father, I'm protecting myself. But I could still call her, couldn't I?

I could, but what would be the point?

She was wrong and she should have offered Malcolm a bed that summer. She shouldn't have made that fuss about the goddamned salmon mousse.

Even so, should I make some move toward a reconciliation?

"Pay attention to the traffic, boss," Coward says.

I don't have to tell him that that's the Coward's way. He'd only answer that I named him and that there's no way I can insult him. I'm rubber; you're glue.

III. Aspects of the Novel

1

The whole idea of a novel is that, one way or another, it tells a story, which is to say it orders events so as to make sense of them – even though, in the world beyond the pages on our lap, there may not be any sense or order. The grand assumptions of narration are quite possibly illusory, but we accept them anyway, because they are what we need to fend off the despair that otherwise tempts and taunts us. Reading novels is not quite the same thing as attendance at our local church or synagogue, but the aims of these activities are oddly congruent. What we want is the faith or courage to get through the trials of the day.

(Faith or courage? One or the other? Ah, I am afraid so.)

And how does the novel do its trick? Often, there is an event, something that just happens, something that falls out of the sky, and if it doesn't rupture the fabric of the fiction (or the fiction of the fabric), then what it offers us is the demonstration we have been looking for of the possibilities of reason – or mere reasonableness – in an arbitrary universe.

There is the knock at the door, the heavy knock at the front door, and there he is, Charles Grandet, Eugénie's cousin, the vain young man whose father, Victor, has failed in business and committed suicide. That's the thing that happens. Or the lawyer announces to Edward Tulliver that the lawsuit has gone badly and that he has lost the water rights to the Floss. Shocked, ruined, he has a stroke, falls off his horse, and for two months suffers from amnesia. The bolt from the blue ...

No, no, no. This isn't a literary essay. I don't believe in literary essays. And I certainly don't believe in theories. What I believe in – at most – are remarks. Is the idea true? Not true?

You decide for yourself, if you care. It could be true, but I'm not all that invested in it. It's the kind of idea that once upon a time could have been the basis of an academic career.

But then, once upon a time, there was a knock at the door, a heavy knock at the front door, and that kind of tweedy pipe-smoking genteel theorizing went out the window.

They took over the classroom, an odd breed of prissy vandals, to whom books present the same kind of challenge as blank walls offer graffiti artists. How can they impose their bizarre notions on the texts and on the readers? "Anal Rape in Jane Austen" is not an absurdist invention of mine but was an actual offering at an MLA meeting a couple of years ago. They compete with one another about who could be the most outrageous, the most provocative, the silliest ...

The jury is still out, and, if they're smart, may never come back.

Anyway, a knock at the door, and who do you think it could be? Who is it always? "It was – ah! – Cool Dan 'n' Rainey Knight!" for whom we are willing to suspend our disbelief.

Suspend it? Hang it! From the highest tree in the county.

But never fear, Dan and Rainey will come along in the nicotine (as good Marlboro men should do?) to shoot the rope from the tree and startle the horse, so that all our put-upon hero has to do is not fall off as his trusty steed gallops away into the sagebrush sunset.

We have our expectations, which may not be great but are clear enough.

But we also know that life isn't a novel, so that when the news comes, we are unprepared. No dustflap copy has warned us; no reviewer has prepared us; no blurbist's ink has offered the least inkling.

If anything has changed, it is merely one's age. The telephone rings, especially at an odd hour, and there is at least the possibility of menace. The angel of death generally telephones, these days.

"Your mother is dead," or "Your father is dead." And the instrument is never quite the same.

"It has happened before?" Dr. Kronkheit asks.

Mr. Dubious admits that, yes, it has happened before.

"So, it's happened again."

"But it hurts when I do this," Dubious says, as the routine continues, making an odd gesture with his arm.

"So, don't do this."

But you can't not answer the phone.

Or, actually, you can. There are people who don't answer the phone, who don't even have phones, just to avoid this kind of call. They are crazy.

But they are not immune from catastrophe, which can come by messenger. Or by mail. The angel will ride hard, if he has to, whipping his horse mercilessly, and he will find you out. And he'll be modest about it, too, rejecting your praise and allowing only that "A man's gotta do what a man's gotta do." That'll be all, Dan. Thank you very much.

I am horsing around here, because I don't want to reenact the ringing of the phone, my picking it up, my recognition of Malcolm's voice – at which, I remember, I actually relaxed, because there wasn't anything menacing about his calling me. But then I realized that I'd been too quick to issue myself that pass and that there was something wrong. His voice didn't have its usual *légèreté*, and I asked him if anything was wrong.

It was his Aunt Alice, he told me. She'd called.

Him? What on earth for? To apologize after all these years? To say that she'd woken up in the middle of the night and realized what a swinish thing it had been for her to turn him away like that when he'd asked to stay with her.

No, that doesn't happen. Not even in novels.

To ask him to deliver a message to me? Yes, of course. It had to be that.

And the message couldn't be good news: I'm feeling fine, and all is well, and I just wanted you to pass that on to my brother who isn't talking to me. Out of the blue, as it were …

What's the matter? I asked. She's sick?

Cancer, Malcolm reported. Lymphoma. Hodgkin's.

Which the hell one is the bad one? Hodgkin's? Non-Hodgkin's?

Whichever one Jackie Kennedy Onassis didn't have is the one you want. Or the one you'd prefer to the other one, which is worse.

Non-Onassis is not a term in common use, though.

I thought for a moment, but then I heard Malcolm's patient breathing on the other end of the line. "And she called you?" I asked.

"To deliver the message to you," he said. "Yes."

"Well, thanks."

Cool Dan doesn't like it. He's the pessimist. His glass is always half empty. And the half that's full has cat piss in it. But he's right, often enough, as he may well be now. He thinks that she made the approach through Malcolm in order to show that he wasn't angry, so I shouldn't be angry either. And she figured that he was a polite enough young man so that he'd be polite and would deliver the message. And he wasn't invested in it, the way I was. He hadn't shared a childhood with his Aunt Alice, never expected much, and therefore hadn't been disappointed the way I was, for his sake, but for my own, as well. It was our childhood together, our parents' assumptions about how people were supposed to behave, and the very idea of family life that she'd trashed. And not incidentally, she'd reminded me of what she'd done to blight the last years of our father's life. Calling Malcolm, she'd managed to get around all that ...

Rainey is ... sunnier. He takes, at any rate, a slightly brighter view, figuring that Alice wasn't all that calculating. She was just afraid of calling me directly. She was frightened and was reaching out to her brother, doing whatever she reckoned had the best chance of working. That's all there is to it.

Maybe, Cool Dan allows, staring into the fire.

After all, Rainey argues, what is she asking? She doesn't need money. She just needs you to be there for her. It's a

terrible phrase, except that that's how she'd put it to herself, because the truth of it is tough to admit – which is
that she wants to be forgiven. Her mother and father are
dead. You're the one who's left.

Of course, that makes me the one who remembers.

It doesn't change anything. What does the news amount to,
after all? That she could die? She will die. I will die. We all
will die. We all scream for ice cream. The great miracle is
that, having evolved these complicated temporal lobes, we
have a sense of time and an awareness of our mortality, as
cats, presumably, do not. And yet we manage to deny it and
live as though we were immortal.

Does our knowledge of our inevitable destiny change
anything? Does it make us behave better? Care more?
Forgive more easily?

A man's gonna do what a man's gonna do, which is
quite different from what John Wayne used to say. And
darker. Dark enough to satisfy Cool Dan at his coldest.

And yet …

We can realize at a certain moment that it isn't just a
general rule but actually applies to us. She knew all along
that she was going to die; now she may find out when this
is actually going to happen. And she is afraid.

Afraid enough, desperate enough to call Malcolm.

One could even construe it as an apology.

You think? Dan asks. Obviously, he doesn't.

Still, he doesn't know everything. How can he, a mere
figment, know more than his creator?

On the other hand, I shouldn't dismiss or patronize
him. Indeed, I wonder whether, in moments of stress, he
may not have figments, too, these irrelevant voices coming

out of nowhere to bedevil him, the minor imps believers
used to imagine in hell, annoying the damned even while
they were undergoing their major torments. It figures, after
all, that hell should be at least as irksome as our lives were,
here on earth.

❖

Consider the alternative. She is not going to die. Not now
and not ever. And neither am I. We are both as immortal
as Cool Dan. Or Zeus and Hera and Ares and Aphrodite,
who were not only fictional but immortal. The Greeks
understood how the immortality of the gods trivialized
them. What men do counts, because we have only one life
and then it ends. The gods go on and on, and if they are
wounded, they ooze a little ichor and then heal up and it
is as if nothing had happened. Nothing can happen. Even
the sufferings of Prometheus are negligible, mathematically.
All those years tied to the rock with the birds pecking at
his liver are frightening to us, but if you take the years and
divide them by infinity, then their proportional significance
turns out to be infinitely small.

The heroes were different: their risks were real and
their losses, terrible.

So it is the lymphoma that puts the question to me in
a more forceful and certainly more pressing way. Can I
continue the estrangement, knowing that she may die in a
year or two and running the risk that I will survive her and
feel guilty for the rest of my life?

Not that I've done anything wrong. She is in the wrong,
I am sure. But how wrong is she? How serious was her
offense? And how long is the sentence to run?

If she'd called to apologize, to admit that she had been
ungenerous and unsisterly, and to beg pardon …

She didn't. Say, even, that she couldn't. Say that she is as proud as she is thoughtless and that she has been angry with me, as people are often angry with those they have wronged. Does this sneaky end-run telephone call to Malcolm erase everything and bring us back to where we were?

And where were we? And when? How far back do we go? To the salmon mousse? The artichoke? The hot dogs at the Log Cabin?

What was attractive about those cowboys was what they never talked about, that chagrin or rage or disgust back East from which they had fled to the wilderness to start over, to create on the high plains or in the hills and canyons a new life that wasn't easier but was as yet untainted by the hypocrisies of civilized life. The namby-pamby storekeeper was always from Philadelphia – a Quaker stronghold, of course. And out there in the clear air and open space, he'd have to learn that there was, indeed, a role for those six-guns. The women, always pacifists, would wring their hands, wipe them on their pretty dimity aprons, and frown disapprovingly, but in the end the hero would see the truth of the proposition that the way to deal with the bad-asses is with cold resolve and hot lead.

It may not be elegant, but in our frustration and despair the showdown has real appeal. The worst that can happen is that you die.

But win or lose, you don't have to go on living with what was intolerable and disgraceful.

What do you want to do, then, shoot her? Shoot your sister? Dan squints out at the mesa in the middle distance.

No, not her. But Kurtz, maybe. Or, even better, both the Kurtzes. It'd be good to bring Joel back, just to shoot him.

He stares at me for a moment and shakes his head. She'd only thank you for it, he says. And you wouldn't be any better off than you are right now.

He's right, of course. But it would feel better. It would be satisfying. If I'm honest with myself, I have to admit that it's a general massacre I want, one of those scenes of mass carnage in the decadent westerns – like the climactic scenes in *Butch Cassidy and the Sundance Kid* or *The Magnificent Seven*.

Like Little Big Horn.

Shoot anything that moves.

2

If depression is rage turned inward, is rage simply depression that has been turned outward?

All this stuff about Kosovars and the Congo, and now Little Big Horn? Where does it tend? What does it mean?

"Who says it has to mean anything, my friend?" It's Leo who is talking, but is not exactly back, because these people don't go away. Let's say, reasserting himself. He's come to America and has established himself here. He's done quite well, actually, parlaying a gypsy cab operation (gypsy cabs and slurpee machines are the two entry-level jobs that hold a mysterious attraction for immigrants) into an entertainment and media empire.

He has a substantial interest in the ice-capade operation that brought such grief to Timmy and Donna, performing a re-enactment of the deplorable Tonya Harding story. Leo also has fast food interests that he has merged with entertainment, buying a number of slaughterhouses in which the customers are able to kill their own food. It started out with just an abattoir and a steak house, but it is the chickens that have done surprisingly well. At New Jersey Fried Chicken, the clerks are dressed as Mafiosi and the customers can cut a bird's throat and watch it die – not necessarily the bird they're going to eat, but chickens look very much alike.

But I am not altogether helpless. I can suppress him, at least for a while. Or humiliate him. I can make bad things happen to him.

Watch.

He has eczema.

He has Dupuytren's contracture, a lump in his palm that isn't malignant but that may eventually cause his ligaments to shrink so that he won't be able to open his fingers all the way. This gives him something to worry about even if all his unattractive and not quite satirical businesses thrive and prosper.

He has toenails disfigured by fungus.

He has gastric reflux so that, if he eats too much at dinner or has wine with dinner or a brandy or even coffee, he has to worry about a horrible burning in his esophagus that will wake him and that may, over time, turn cancerous.

See?

But none of this helps me or makes me feel any better.

Back, is he? Like a bad penny. He has taken a vacation, has perhaps been taking the waters at Bad Pfennig, we may even imagine. With such an array of minor ailments, that would be as reasonable a way as any for him to have spent his time. But even there, he was on call, as characters in novels always are.

What he will make of this latest development, where we seem to have been thinking about the old west and the Indians, is not immediately clear, but presumably he knows the novels of Karl May, and therefore he probably has his views.

May was that petty crook who took to writing, mostly because all other avenues of employment were closed to him. And he spun yarns, knock-off versions of James Fenimore Cooper, that entertained Albert Einstein and Herman Hesse when they were kids.

Also Adolf Hitler, who was a big fan.

The fact that young Adolph used to read May's novels has tainted their reputation somewhat, probably unfairly. May's tales of Winnetou and Old Shatterhand are not only innocent but stupid. Dim genre writing. James Fenimore Cooper, from whom he is derivative, is too literary and highbrow to be a useful comparison. Think rather of Zane Grey. Or Louis L'Amour.

May's Indians are noble savages, picturesque but doomed. And the fate that awaits them is to be driven from the paradise they could no more understand and appreciate than Adam and Eve understood theirs. What displaces them is civilization, or, to be blunt about it, us. And we are not so much participants as fans. Rooters.

We sit in our Lazy-boys, munch microwave popcorn, and watch the game between the Yankees and the Braves. Or the Cowboys and the Redskins.

It has been suggested that Hitler got the idea of the final solution of the Jewish problem from the novels of Karl May. It may be true. But May isn't responsible for Hitler's "strong misreading."

Or not altogether responsible.

What's scary is how pop-lit can turn around and bite us in the ass, with all those dopey ideas fermenting so that, under the right conditions, they can affect susceptible minds.

It's the law of unintended consequences. Universal literacy is a dangerous experiment, leading not to general betterment but to catastrophe. With all those people who know how to read but don't know how to think, what you've had since the last half of the nineteenth century is an incubator of social and political unrest. And literary corruption, too, because, not surprisingly, these great hordes are also deficient in taste and refinement.

They know how to read but they don't do it well, which is worse than their not reading at all.

Do I really think this? Or am I just being disagreeable?

How can I possibly tell?

The worst case is that I'm correct and also crazy, which is therefore likely. It's the paranoid's nightmare, anyway.

The worst case is that Malcolm and Joanne are to be married. And that while I was hurt and angry at Alice's absence from his graduation from law school, I will now have to assent to her being invited to the wedding, and her presence will be even more hurtful and infuriating.

As any hot dog can tell you, "Out of the wurst case and into the frying pan."

It's Joanne's parents' party, but we get to decide about who gets invited from our side. Alice, if I'm talking to her, ought to be invited.

Andouille? We do, I'm afraid.

But good grief! A wedding?

Back when I was a kid, when there were double and triple features at the movies, you just went, any time, and you sat there until you recognized scenes you'd seen before, which was the signal that it was time to get up and leave.

We've seen this before. But there's no way to get up and walk out into the dazzle of daylight.

I called. I figured it was as awkward for her as for me, but it probably wasn't. I was thinking about history. She was looking towards an obnubilated and perhaps drastically diminished future. It is a curious eschatological question as to whether the business of dying is in itself unpleasant enough to redeem our lives and erase our sins. The prospect of death is supposed to prompt repentance in our hearts, even if momentary. But is that necessary? The fact that a life and a self are to be extinguished may be, all by itself, a harsh enough punishment.

Ah, but what about the virtuous people, if there are any?

But who knows what was going on in Alice's mind? Our call was peculiarly correct, as if it would have been some kind of lapse of decorum had either of us mentioned that the interval between this and our previous conversation must have been ... Six years? Seven?

No reference to that, of course. And relatively little talk about her lymphoma, which is still being evaluated. She is to hear the doctors' proposed treatment plan in a couple of days.

> So, what else was there to talk about?
> And how is the pussycat?
> And how is the dog?
> Oh, oh,
> I am so glad you called,
> I was just thinking of you,
> Yes. No, I'm not feeling very well ...

It's Menotti. From "The Telephone," I think. I cite it here because its sappiness suggested itself, and it was with some difficulty that I kept myself from singing that passage to her while we were on the phone.

She had no way of knowing this. As I had no way of knowing what was in her mind. I can't even begin to guess. What can it be like for a woman whose father didn't talk to her for twenty years to hear from a brother who hasn't talked to her for seven, to discuss her diagnosis of lymphoma?

In all that time, had she ever wondered whether we were right and sane, while she was wrong and crazy?

She is not, so far as I can tell, a sociopath, which is to say that she admits that other people are real. We aren't all automatons put here to test, amuse, or annoy her. As if we were secondary characters in novels, that is.

Each of us – I do believe she thinks – has a certain Kantian dignity.

But I have no idea.

And for me to suppose the best of her – that she, too, was thinking of the Menotti piece but couldn't say so – wouldn't change anything.

"You'll let me know," I told her, about the treatment plan.

Five years ago, five days ago, my treatment plan would have been to put her out on an ice floe and let her drift off into the Bering Sea.

But that was a fantasy and this is real.

"I'll let you know," she says. And then, at last, she asks what's really on her mind. "Will I see you?"

What can I say? It was foregone, the moment I made the call, wasn't it?

Sure. Soon.

And then I realize that I have thought it but I have to say it, too. And it's as if I have to say it again!

"Sure. Soon," I manage in a voice that sounds almost normal.

"Good," she says.

Each of us waits for the other to say something more, but it doesn't happen. Is that a disappointment or a relief?

Not only do I have no idea what's going on in her head, I'm not even sure what's going on in my own.

Should I mention the wedding? I'd decided to save that for another call, letting it have that dignity and importance. But I'm uncomfortable enough so that it's tempting.

But I resist.

"I'll call you, then," she says.

"Do that."

And then, when I've lowered the phone halfway back to the cradle, I hear – I think I hear – "Thanks."

3

It's a matter of punctuation as much as anything else. I remember once seeing a sign at some summer resort where there was a lemonade stand that said, "Fresh Lemonade" – just like that, in quotes. For emphasis, maybe. Or to suggest that it was really really fresh. But whatever the intention was, the effect to those few passersby who were literate was "wink, wink, nudge, nudge, it isn't fresh at all, even if we're saying so, because the quotes leach out all the authority of the claim and reduce it to a phrase we've all seen before that may or may not apply."

And Alice will be there, my sister, but in quotes, because everyone there will be aware of the history. They'll all be perfectly well aware that she is not just Malcolm's aunt and my sister who of course would be there. She's also the sister I haven't talked to for years, but whom I've invited now because of my sentimentality or my sheer lack of character.

In the crunch, I crumped. I caved in to weakness majeure.

They'll know, some of them anyway, about the lymphoma, and that may be an excuse, but the quotes will be there, over all our heads. "Proud father" next to the "proud mother," who can't stand each other. And "estranged sister who has been allowed back because she is bravely battling this dread disease ..."

Why do they always say that those with cancer are battling it "bravely"?

But that's in quotes, too.

❖

Instead of contemplating what will surely be another occasion of deep chagrin where, at best, I will not have allowed any of the guests on the other side of the aisle to see how uncomfortable I am, I will be off in my cloud-cuckooland of grotesque refuge.

For which, presumably, I could make better preparation this time than I have before.

As Dr. Kronkheit says to Mr. Dubious, "You had it before? You've got it again!" A lot of life's wisdom is like that, so obvious that we're embarrassed not to have seen it before.

One of the great differences between novels and life is that in a novel, at a time of stress, if the character is going to bug out with some kind of fantasy, the author has as long as he wants to think up something pointed and poignant, apposite and entertaining ... He can lie there on the daybed, listen to Vivaldi, and stare at the ceiling, waiting for something to occur to him.

In life, the poor son of a bitch is there, at the graduation or the funeral, and has to make do with whatever pops up in his preoccupied mind.

So the author, if he's honest, should go with whatever his first thought was, however stupid, because that's what life in the world is like. And novels are supposed to be a representation of a shared and recognizable reality.

But there's no reason the character can't prepare himself better, knowing what's likely to happen. It's less than spontaneous, but people go around with Viagra in their pillboxes or condoms in their wallets, in the hope that an occasion may, if you'll pardon the expression, arise.

Ah, well.

Indians, is it? Karl May and Custer, and all that?

Why? Because, frankly, they piss me off. They're an affront to the Constitution. The idea that they have an ethnic right to run casinos, a racial entitlement to operate businesses that are, for all other citizens of the United States, illegal, is a violation of the fundamental principle that all men are equal under the law. It's affirmative action times ten. It's outrageous.

Or one could put it the other way, and ask, more quietly, why not?

And it connects, I'm afraid. Whatever else a novel may be about, it is also inevitably about the novel, which is to say civilization. And the Indians used to be the defining limit of that. The noble savage is an idea (Chateaubriand's?) that arises from fatigue or even disgust with the claims of civilized life, which is so often uncivil. After the Balkans and Africa, where else is there to go but the last frontier, where Winnetou rides bareback, and, for all I know, bare-ass, through the sea of grass of the high prairie.

Him plenty tough Injun.

You're not allowed to say that kind of thing anymore, that pidgin redskin talk Tonto used with the Lone Ranger. It's politically incorrect, but that makes it attractive, and even, in some ways, compulsory.

Jay Silverheels didn't seem to mind. He was the Indian who played Tonto. Made a good living at it. Plenty fine gig. Better, anyway, than selling pots and blankets to tourists in Albuquerque.

They're supposed to have been sensitive to the ecology, which is so much buffalo kaka. They just didn't have the technological knowhow to fuck it up.

As between political incorrectness and historical inaccuracy, you've got to make your choice. Which path to take.

Winnetou gets off his horse, kneels down, sniffs the dirt, picks up a glob of horseshit, and smells it.

"Him go this way," he says, pointing nobly toward the west.

How does he know?

He doesn't. He's guessing.

Then what was that stuff with the horseshit?

He just likes smelling horseshit. It's so … primitive and ecological.

Ugh.

❖

And where does the path lead, you may reasonably ask. Not even the sappiest romantic has ever attributed to them any particular talent for figure skating.

No, maybe not, but they have these casinos, right? And they have to have entertainment to bring the suckers in, right?

So Leo has booked Timmy and Donna into Wampum Lodge, a casino operated by the Paskudniac tribe in upper lower Michigan.

It could break your heart, the things these kids have to put up with. But as Leo says to his dejected clients, there are worse bookings.

The things one has to do for art's sake.

(Art? Leo's partner? No!)

❖

What's attractive about the Indians is that they are Unter-
menschen. They are therefore the obvious targets of liberal
interest. Liberals are always wanting to go out there and
improve the lot of their fellow man, and, now that it has
been decided that Indians are human beings (it really was
an open philosophical and theological question a couple of
hundred years ago), they are, even more than the blacks,
the natural objects of liberal concern. The blacks may have
been carried away in chains and brought to these shores,
but the Indians were already here and were displaced from
their rightful home.

Rightful, of course, is the tricky word. They didn't have
any sense of property. The idea of ownership – which left-
ists deplore anyway – was foreign to them.

We, the foreigners, brought it and imposed it.

Property is theft. But they couldn't have thought any
such thing without an idea of property. And an idea of theft.

They understand property better now, of course.
Without it, their damned casinos make no sense at all.

Of course, they'd be a lot more fun. You could gamble
for a week, lose a couple of thousand, and then, at the end,
just shrug and say there was no such thing as property. And
they'd look at you with nobility and calm and nod to the
Russian gangster to go after you and either work out a
payment plan or break your legs for you.

Meanwhile, they've got their waitresses and bartend-
ers dressed up in buckskin miniskirts and sporting head-
bands with feathers, get-ups that would be outrageous and
condescending if the proprietors weren't, themselves,
Indians. It's Disney with tits. Although, come to think of
it, Disney's babes are usually pretty well endowed. His
cartoon cuties are not at all wanting in the tits-and-ass
department. (And it isn't inadvertent. Nothing in that busi-

ness just happens. There's an audience for it, and income to be earned.)

Will Dan and Rainey cross trails with Winnetou and his Paskudniac war party? Will they be ambushed? Or bushwhacked? Will they be taken captive and brought back to camp at the Wampum Casino to be tortured by the chorus of squaws in the last scene of the ice capades, while Timmy and Donna look on helplessly, and Leo shakes his head and wishes he were back in Kosovo, where it was horrible but at least familiar and coherent?

I certainly hope not.

But I fear the wurst.

4

Alice's news is mixed. She will be having chemotherapy, which sounds menacing. It's a clinical locution for poison, after all. But the oncologist was relatively optimistic and said that the chances of a remission were excellent.

Or, to drop the code words they use, they can almost certainly buy her some time and may even be able to cure her, cure being a more or less amorphous idea, the main qualification being that you're symptom free and die of something else. All things considered, that's not such a bad deal.

But she's scared. Stunned, really. And I can't blame her for that.

I am, meanwhile, thinking of what it meant for her to telephone me and for me then to hear her voice on the machine and call her back. Am I betraying my father? Assuming that the dead are capable of being betrayed, that they're aware of what's going on with us, and that they are still carrying grudges, would he disapprove?

I never heard our mother discuss this. It never came up, not even between the time that my father died and her own death some years later. I always assumed it was too personal. Or it was one of those distressing things that she would have thought in poor taste to discuss openly.

But under the pressure of the moment, on the phone with Alice, asking her the questions and negotiating our way through the mine of taboo subjects, I realized that there might have been a tacit understanding between my parents. My father might very well have wanted her to keep in touch with Alice, because she was still their daughter and he still loved her.

It was a bitter pill that, as with some cakes, you could eat and have too.

That gag is terrible, but the truth behind it was terrible.

One phrase she used, though, is worth some contemplation. At one point I heard her say that she felt her body had "betrayed" her.

It's the kind of idea that would have been at home in Dad's head. He had, as she discovered, ideas of duty and honor and, conversely, of betrayal.

And his body, at last, betrayed him. Everyone's does.

We think of our bodies as our own, as possessions, or maybe as junior partners. But they have their own will, as any dieter can tell you. And their own destiny, as your doctor will make clear to you one day.

They go about their business in their slow, dim way, letting us think that we can go where we want, do what we want, and that they will take orders from our minds, more or less as machines do – if, indeed, we think of them as having a separate identity at all.

But they do have separate identities. Suicide is the decision of the mind not to put up with the outrageous perseveration of the lungs' bellows and the heart's pumping. Enough, the spirit says, and there are pills or bullets, or high windows.

The poor dumb body does what it has been told to do and the rest of us are appalled.

But the contrary story happens every day. The spirit is busy with projects, work, family, culture, and all the rest of what we think of as the good things of life, and the body has had it. It turns away, defying us whether by an act of will or merely because it has a destiny we had never imagined. And the signs of its turning are there for the radiologist or the surgeon to read.

We are, when such a thing happens, more or less appalled. Some of us may be inured, like the Kosovars, having seen too many horror scenes to react with any particular energy anymore. We may, some of us, turn fatalists.

Sniper fire, grenades, occasional mortars in the neighborhoods we walk through every day, and they're not at all remarkable. We need a liter of milk or a loaf of bread, and off we go through the chaos – bravely or stupidly – to make our modest and mundane purchases.

One would think we were in some mall with security guards, plashing fountains, and elaborate plantings.

Where, of course, you can have a heart attack or a stroke, or choke on a piece of your sandwich and keel over, dead.

There isn't any betrayal because there was never any promise to be broken or faith to be betrayed.

Except as a fiction.

In a novel, no matter what the author has in mind, the reader can feel with the thumb of his right hand that diminution of heft as the unread pages dwindle down. There is a sense of the finite. There is closure. Characters may die, but the book will go on, and we can look to see how many pages are left and how much time remains. Freud's idea of the death instinct was altogether batty and difficult to account for, but my guess is that what he wanted was for lives to have the shapeliness of novels. The only way for that to happen is through misrepresentation: life – or nature – isn't like that.

Of course, there are opportunities, such as the one Alice now has. Reminded in this way of her mortality, she could consider some startling and yet altogether logical gesture that would give her life the shapeliness of a work of art. She could take this oncological prompting as an ontological opportunity. She could exploit the opportunities of the coincidence of her diagnosis and Malcolm and Joanne's wedding to contrive some resolution – some correction of the direction and meaning of her life.

A lot of short stories work that way, and some novels, too. There is an exposition and then a correction, and the not-this-but-that allows us to participate in the discovery and to experience the growth and change that is what narrative art is about. These swaths of prose are not presentations of the authors' wisdom but representations of the emotions that are sometimes attendant upon its acquisition.

On the other hand, there is the epiphany story, in which nothing happens except that the reader has a small ah-ha experience. Or the Salinger story, which has its own weird structure. There's a wound, and the protagonist or the narrator wonders whether it still hurts. There's a probe somehow, and, the answer is, yes, it still hurts.

And we recognize that, yes, that's how life is, because we have wounds that still hurt and that will always hurt.

It could be that Alice will come to the wedding just to demonstrate that it still hurts. Her and me.

Maybe she's thinking all this and deciding, after all, not to come. She has got this terrific (in both senses) excuse, after all. She could be content to have been invited. And she could show a certain tact and decency and send not only an extravagant present but an even more lavish absence, or, more simply put, her regrets.

Regrets? Aren't they exactly what I want from her?

She isn't troubled by them, herself, I'm afraid. But she is a carrier.

5

The dinner, which I dreaded, goes well enough. I don't implode. And I don't break up, either, into uncontrollable laughter. Joanne's earnest and businesslike uncles, her mother's brothers, are Shelley and Milton and Byron, and I did not laugh. All of these used to be plausible names for Jews whose goal was assimilation. That was a generation or two ago, of course. But inasmuch as Jews name infants after deceased relatives, the names refuse to disappear.

I can imagine the arguments when these uncles were born, the terms of which are obvious enough. Should they continue with the English poets, Joanne's grandparents wondered? Or should they revert to the original forms of the names – Shmuel, Moshe, and Baruch? I have the advantage of seeing them as grown-ups, but I can't begin to guess which way they'd have been less uncomfortable, as children, as adolescents, or now.

My own preference would have been for the biblical forms, if only because these men are so aggressively, so strenuously unpoetic. But then I recognize that I did not prevail against a preference as strong as Nina's, for instance. I couldn't hold out for Meshullam and I wouldn't have been able to resist this extravagance either.

It could have been worse, I guess. If their parents had been admirers of Alexander Pope and had had another son, he might have been in real trouble.

But it's a game now, isn't it? Spenser is possible. And Blake. And ... Vaughan!

Irrelevant to their situation, but irrelevance is my domain.

I am not, in any of this, spiteful. They seem pleasant enough, Joanne's relatives. On their good behavior anyway. As I am. As we all are, most of the time. Which is heart-breaking, if you think about it. How much worse would the world be if most of us weren't trying to behave well?

The details of the dinner were painless enough. The restaurant Malcolm found had a "function room," which sounds as though it has more to do with plumbing than eating. Banquet, I expect, is too highfalutin' and off-putting. I told Malcolm to pick out whatever he and Joanne wanted for the food, which saved me having to deal with Nina.

Not that I am able to make decisions so easily, myself. I get along perfectly well for days, for weeks at a time, and

then, for no particular reason, find that, in the aisles of a
supermarket, I am unable to make choices about what to
buy for dinner. It can happen in restaurants, too, but I have
a system there. If I find myself paralyzed, I can make an
arbitrary selection, picking the third thing from the bottom
in each category.

Malcolm and Joanne did the seating plan. Alice and I
were at the first table, across from Nina and Allen, so that
there was the least possible occasion for conversation –
unless we were to shout, which would not have been unprecedented. Separating us, was a large floral display, and
ranged around the table between us, like diplomats from
neutral countries, were the bridal couple; Joanne's parents,
Bill and Karyn; Jason and Caroline; Joanne's sister, Fleur,
with some young man who was her date but whose name
and condition I never got; and Bill's brother, Herman, and
his wife, Claire.

You don't get many Hermans these days. Goering
killed the name, I should suppose, as Hitler and Eichmann
caused a decline in the popularity of Adolf.

From these names, one would think that both sides of
Joanne's family must have spent some years in a time
capsule, where they'd been resting in industrial popcorn,
untouched by time or culture.

I'm being unfair and judgmental. Or, more accurately,
judgmental. There's nothing unfair about it, because it is
not paranoid of me to imagine that they're making such
judgments about me. There may not be any stigma, these
days, that attaches to being divorced, but these people are
not living in "these days." They seem to be Kaufman and
Hart characters trying to pass as Normal Rockwell models.
And I can imagine that they are displeased that Malcolm's
family has not survived.

And to people like that, divorce is not so much a sign of immorality as a defect in interior decoration. It is as if those connoisseurs on *Antiques Roadshow* had taken a hard look at us and shaken their heads in disapproval because the exterior had been refinished and there were parts that weren't original.

Having thought of this, and having attributed it to Joanne's family, I feel defensive, but I'm not sure that I don't agree with them. It's my own idea, after all. None of them has uttered a peep.

On the other hand, if they're as sharp as I am afraid they may be, they know they don't have to.

What I mostly remember about the dinner is that I didn't remember much. What stunned me was Alice in her turban, which was supposed to conceal her drastically thinning hair, but which gave her a peculiarly ecclesiastic and other-worldly look. It was as if she had taken leave from some cloister, interrupting her regimen of prayer and meditation to keep us company on this great occasion, while also reminding us what is eternal and important.

She had lost weight, and the bones of her face were somehow more prominent, as if the skull beneath the skin were signaling to us that it would soon put by the rags of the flesh to emerge in the ghastly whiteness to which, all along, it had aspired. I didn't say any of this, of course. What I said to her was that she was looking less bad than I'd feared. And she'd thanked me for what she called a "cali-brated compliment."

It would be disappointing in a novel, but was altogether satisfactory in real life, that her gaunt and raddled look subdued me enough to prevent trivial disasters. Nobody said

anything strange or provocative enough to drive me into
the wilderness of the high plains, where my savages are
always on the warpath. I was subdued, shocked, chastened
enough to be able to function as well as anyone else in the
function room. At least for a few hours, I was what a more
or less normal person would seem to be under such circumstances. Joanne may not be the most exciting woman in the
world, but that may be a good thing. She and Malcolm may
wear better and last longer than Nina and I were able to. I
think we talked a little about Italy, where Malcolm and
Joanne would be traveling for their honeymoon, and I was
interested, eager to be helpful but without showing off.
Alice spoke about Sicily, where she'd visited some years
before. Malcolm and Joanne wouldn't be going there, not
on this trip anyway, but another time ... And I couldn't help
thinking that their notion of the future was open-ended,
as it is for most of us. But not for Alice. Not anymore.

But whether it was Alice's presence, or my own state
of mind, which is, most of the time, precariously anchored,
the evening was unreal, which is, of course, what many real
things aspire to be. Alice's presence there with me was
supposed to "balance the table," and it did, but not in the
way any party planner could have imagined.

I doubt that anyone was keeping score. I wasn't, myself. But without Alice there, I might very well have felt
outnumbered. She and I were avoiding any reference to an
issue so large that our estrangement seemed unimportant.
For whatever reason, we seemed to have contrived, without any coordination or consultation, a way of speaking and
behaving as if nothing had ever been wrong, as if we had
been talking regularly, once or twice a week on the telephone, the way normal brothers and sisters do – if any such
people exist.

Ronnie wasn't there, however. Not invited, I assume. But his absence was a kind of presence, a companionable deficiency, because I knew that, if she'd had her druthers, Nina would have had my name crossed off the list, too. Even to this, to my own party.

Druthers? It's another instance of tmesis, and we have the great satisfaction of having spotted it in the wild.

What was remarkable, however, was that, aside from such fleeting thoughts, my mind was mostly there, where I was, attending upon external reality, as good obedient minds ought to do. No ice skaters, no Indians. No Kosovar guerillas. No African traders or other deplorable flights of fancy.

I do remember thinking, as the dinner party broke up, that I might actually be able to get through this whole event. The evening had begun well. The next day there'd be the ceremony, and then the lunch, and then the cutting of the cake, and the newlyweds would take off, as, a few nanoseconds later, would I.

Of course, there was always the possibility that this was only a set-up.

We all know the lines. Cool Dan says something about how it's quiet out there.

And Rainey shakes his head, maybe spits, and says, "Too quiet."

And then a thousand war-painted Paskudniacs come pouring down from the ridge, riding bareback, and almost deafening us with their blood-curdling screams.

From which the obvious lesson is to be drawn: never let down your guard.

❖

The wedding went the way weddings go, if perhaps more lavishly and showily than was absolutely necessary, but I could hardly blame Bill and Karyn for exploiting the occasion just a bit to show off for their friends. Isn't this what my father wanted to do? Sure, there were a few friends of the bride and of the groom, and there we were, the members of the groom's family, but mostly it was Bill and Karyn's party, and they were having a good time, marking the milestone, almost making a monument of it. The only thing that jarred, just a little, was the great swarm of photographers. There was a videotaping crew, and there was a still photographer with his assistants. And Uncle Herman, with both a digital camera and a film camera, was taking pictures, too. At one point, he was taking shots of the still photographers who were recording the video camera operators at work.

Very intellectual. Almost perverse.

Or allowing that it was a perfectly acceptable and predictable practice, one could still begin to wonder, at a certain point, where the primary experience was actually located. Was it here, at the wedding, or at some future time, when, in Bill and Karyn's living room, there would be the glossies in the album, or the slides, or the videotapes, or the images on the computer's hard drive that would flicker on one screen or another for guests, who would recognize themselves and, if they have any social savvy, volubly admire? The wedding itself was merely the ore from which those presentations were to be extracted and refined.

It was as if we had all had been turned into Japanese tourists.

❖

Or I will be more generous, more empathetic. Let me suppose that they are not altogether persuaded that they are alive, in which case they need the record, the contact sheet and the album pages, and even the record of the record – these still pictures of the photographers taking shots of the videocamera crew. What is being strenuously asserted is that the event, the wedding, is real, is important, must be important to have all this attention lavished upon it.

And of course the opposite effect is what they achieve, but that doesn't mean that their efforts are despicable. Sad, perhaps, but not contemptible.

My own mental state was not especially worrisome. I seemed, at the wedding, to be managing myself well enough. Alice and I were sitting next to each other, and then beyond Alice there were Allen and Nina, and Nina's Uncle Jack. And then, obviously by accident, an empty seat, the Siege Perilous, Ronnie's seat.

Or my father's?

No, not at all. And I mustn't allow myself to go that way. Alice is here and I'm here, and our parents are dead and not worrying about any of this anymore.

Besides, it isn't my father that I'm thinking about. He's a more comfortable diversion. That black hole, the gravitational pull of which I've been trying to resist, is my presence at Jason's wedding.

Samantha and I were still together. But the deal was that Nina wouldn't come if Samantha was there. So I was invited and Samantha wasn't. Nina was there, with Allen, but I had the choice of either staying away or of showing up and looking like a fool and a loser.

And, of course, if I stayed away, my mother, who was still alive, would have had to stay away, too.

So I swallowed my pride and I agreed to this outrageousness.

Jason was sorry about it, but that's what his mother had told him: he was just delivering the message.

And then, at the wedding itself, there was some horrible business about the chairs in the first row, where members of the immediate family were to sit.

A moment's thought might have avoided this awkwardness, but they had other things to think about.

Anyway, the question came suddenly as to whether Allen, to whom Nina was not yet married, was to sit in the front row or just behind her in the second row.

And I said, sounding more like Nina than I expected I could, "If he sits in the first row, I'm leaving."

My mother glared at me, horrified.

And I told her the truth. "I'm sorry," I said quietly. "I can't help myself."

Literally, I could not. And she believed me, because she could hear in my voice not the anger she had learned to endure from my father, but fear, because I knew I was altogether out of control. It was an appalling sensation, that awful out-of-time moment between the slipping of the crystal goblet from out of the hand and the inevitable consequence of its expensive shattering on the hard floor far below.

Allen, who is not a vicious fellow, didn't say anything, but, either out of courtesy or concern, let me have my way and took a seat in the second row.

We could continue. But I knew how close I'd come to a disgrace worse than my father's.

He wasn't responsible for what his daughter had done. No one could have supposed so. His daughter had embarrassed him, but he had not embarrassed or disgraced himself. At Jason's wedding, it would have been assumed that I was sane and I would have been thought responsible for walking out, dragging my mother after me, ruining the occasion …

We think we are leading our lives. More likely and more terrifying, we must admit to the possibility that they are leading us. Although we can perhaps influence our destinies a little, here and there, they have their own direction, their own impetus, their own logic.

Or their own madness.

Which is why I was checking my status. Even a relatively un-seaworthy craft can get across the cove on a calm day.

The photographers were snapping away, doing their work. I remember thinking that one of them, a gaunt-looking woman with severe salt-and-pepper hair and an impressive array of cameras dangling from her neck, looked particularly grim. It was a wedding, after all, but she could have been taking snapshots of a Mafia funeral for the files of the FBI. Her lips were pursed, perhaps in concentration, as she framed shots and considered the light, the speed of the film, and those technical matters. But her expression, when she was disgusted or enraged, would not have been discernibly different.

I remember noting this and being amused by it.

The ability to notice things and to be amused by them is healthy, isn't it? That's being connected to the world. And, at that instant anyway, I was.

Comes then the rabbi, ready to blow up the lungs of chickens and declare that they are glatt kosher, wave his hands over the bride and groom, consecrate their union, and mutter the prayers of our people. Decked out with war paint on his face, feathered from head to heel, and dangling powerful amulets of antelope horn and buffalo pizzle, he chants to the great spirit and expresses our collective wish that as long as the grass grows and the wind blows, we shall smoke our pipe of peace and make no more war forever, until we have reached the happy hunting ground where all good Paskudniacs eventually go.

I forget which Indian chief it was during those wars, but one of them moved his people north and across the border so that he could surrender not to the Americans, whom he knew to be faithless, but to the Royal Canadian Mounted Police, whose red uniforms were designed to be impressive to savages and who had not so flagrantly broken their word to other defeated chieftains.

Maybe we should have a Mountie reciting the prayers and offering the appropriate blessings. This, after all, was the ceremony that united Nina and me. And Alice and Harvey.

Them plenty bad for rain dance, keemosabee, Winnetou says, and Cool Dan agrees with him.

My face is a mask, impassive as that of your wooden Indian out in front of the cigar store, standing out there in the weather and taking whatever solace he can in the thought that some of those cigars are the trick-shop items that explode.

The wedding. It was a wedding. You don't need me to describe a wedding, do you? You've all been to weddings. It was a perfectly unremarkable wedding, even though the photographers were making it look like a shoot for some product that we only find out about at the end of the commercial.

I behaved myself. I traded with the Indians. I counted breaths. I even went back to my most drastic stratagem, conjugating *luo*, the paradigmatic Greek verb, which runs on as all Greek verbs do, and which makes me uneasy because there are always forms that I've forgotten. *Luo, lueis, luei*, for I loose, you loose, he looses, and *lueton*, and *lueton*, for the two of you loose, and the two of them loose, the dual being appropriate for pairs like Agamemnon and Menelaus, or Castor and Pollux. And *luomen, luete, luousi*, for we loose, you all loose, and they loose. Easy enough, but then there are the imperfect and the future, as well as the subjunctive, the optative, the imperative, and, of course, the middle voice – I loose for myself, or I loose myself – and so on. It's enough to produce a panicky feeling, so that I am unaware of the other, exterior panic. It is like being back in class in prep school and not well prepared, and terrified that I am about to be called on and will, yet again, make a fool of myself. Or, more accurately, be shown up as a fool. Unable to loose myself.

It is, I am perfectly well aware, a counter-irritant. It is a mental TENS machine, which stands for transcutaneous electronic neuron stimulator, I think. Arthritics wear those, relying on a series of electric shocks to the skin to confuse the nervous system so that it can't deliver to the brain the more serious protests from the hip or the knee or whatever is really out of order and in need of assistance.

Assistance? Narcotics, more like.

Lusasthon! Loose for yourselves, you two. That doesn't come up a whole lot, I'll tell you. But if it ever did, that would be the dual imperative and that's what it would look like.

What I look like is ... concentrating. Thoughtful. As if I were thinking about my son and my daughter-in-law-to-be. Or already? Are they done already?

Evidently so. Chief Winnetou is raising his hands. The groom is breaking the ceremonial glass. He will pick her up, fling her across his pinto pony, and ride off with her to the wigwam to consummate the union, while the rest of us dance, get drunk, and show off by giving expensive presents.

I made it. Congratulations!

6

And then the incident, which isn't, I must warn you, all that much of a big deal. Or it wouldn't have been to someone else. But I was stretched to my limit, was working with very little margin, and if the slightest thing will set you off, then some slight thing is likely to come along, as if it had been waiting, as if it had been plotted, as if everything that had been happening were preparation for this.

A small thing? Well, like that guy in the red tie who gets killed because the two punks have agreed that that's whom they're going to hit ... Small, but not altogether insignificant.

The bride and the groom walk down the aisle together, and then the rabbi, and then the wedding party, with the bride's parents first, and then Nina and Allen, and then Alice and me. And the other guests, all the aunts and uncles and the bride's grandmother, and then the friends and the other guests. And we all make our way to the table in the reception area where there's a goblet of wine and an enormous challah set out for the blessings that will initiate the feast. We're gathered around the table, behind which the bride and groom and the rabbi are standing, with Bill and Karyn flanking them, and there are a lot of people in a not terribly well designed space, so that those in the back are crowding forward to try to see. And because it's a predictable and photogenic moment, the photographers are intruding themselves with particular energy, because they've got to have this shot, which isn't quite the breaking of the glass or the cutting of the cake, but it's up there, and it's something that the families will expect to see on the contact sheets.

I understand all that. I do now and probably did then. A degree of pressure is on these picture takers, who are not just having a good time, but are trying to make a living. And yet, it is also true that they are not, themselves, the event, but only the recorders of the event. What's happening is that the bride and groom are going to sip the wine and cut into the bread and that we're going to watch and say "Amen" when they recite the blessings.

So when that gaunt woman with salt-and-pepper hair and the grim look and the array of cameras comes up behind me and, without saying anything, not a word, not "Excuse me" or "I beg your pardon," or any other civil signal, but merely grabs me and shoves me to one side so that she can get her shot, I feel … Assaulted? Yes, but not severely, not physically hurt. Surprised, I guess. Startled, even. And then, a couple of nanoseconds later, shocked. I mean, what the hell? This is no way to treat a guest. This is no way to treat the groom's father. This is no way to treat a human being.

I am not a potted plant. I am part of this. I am not a thing you move around because it happens to be in the way.

I have a feeling of helpless rage welling up from deep, deep within. From my father, even, who did not have to endure his humiliation in public this way but could go to bed and pull the covers over his head and lie there in the darkness.

Alice, of course, is beside me. Has she seen what happened? Has she thought of her own wedding? Perhaps so, but has she thought of Dad in a dark room, furious and hurt? Probably not. For her sake, I hope not.

But this is intolerable.

They're clicking away, she and the others, as the bride and groom hold the pose with the silver goblet between them, and I take advantage of the opportunity by saying to her, quietly but clearly enough so that I'm sure she can hear, because she's right beside me, "You touch me again, and I'll deck you."

She turns, looks at me, glares – or I think she glares. Her expression was more or less glaring in repose. And then she turns away and brings the eyepiece of the camera back to her face. Click, click, click.

The blessing over the bread. The blessing over the wine.

And during this time, I'm reasoning with myself. I'm being fair. I'm arguing on the glowering woman's behalf, proposing to myself that she didn't realize what she was doing ...

But it wasn't an inadvertent shove. She was perfectly well aware of what she was doing.

Even so, what I said, what I heard myself saying, was crude, too, although it was only words, while what she did was, technically, a battery.

At the first opportunity, which is right after the "Amen" from the guests, I tell her, "You can't just shove people around like that," meaning it, I thought then and think now, as halfway toward an apology.

"You can't threaten women like that," she snaps back.

And one of the videotaping guys says, "You lay a hand on her, buddy, and you'll have me to deal with."

"Are you threatening me?" I ask.

"I'm just telling you how it is, pal."

For a guy like him, "pal" is an insult, but this is not the time to explore the semantic implications of that.

What was, until that moment, fluid, has now suddenly set, has turned hard as concrete. And my feet are encased in it.

No hope. No escape. No way out. I cannot loose myself.

Shoot anything that moves.

I can't stay in the same room with them. Can't and won't.

It becomes clear what I must do. Which is not altogether a good sign. People who respond to such cues are either like St. Joan or else they are put away in padded rooms, in those stylish white coats with sleeves that tie in the back.

But I have no choice, which means that I don't have the burdensome business of deciding. As if under orders, I go to Bill and tell him: "I'm sorry to make trouble at a time like this, but I've been assaulted."

"What?"

"That photographer, who is in your employ, pushed me. Intentionally. As if I were a piece of furniture that was in the way."

"She couldn't have meant it."

"She meant it."

There is a pause. He is thinking about this. He is thinking that this is the last thing he wants to be thinking about.

"What do you want me to do?" he asks.

"Get rid of her. Send her away."

"I can't do that."

I see the next line and don't want to say it. But the alternative is that I leave without saying it, without even giving him the chance. And although I know that he won't appreciate it, it is for his sake that I force myself to say, in as unthreatening and as pleasant a way as I can manage, "Either she leaves or I do."

"That's up to you."

There is a fist clenching my heart. It is a horrible cliché, but I can feel it and it is not merely a figure of speech. There is a tightness in my chest that is literal, physical.

"I'm a guest," I say, very softly and with more regret than menace, because I know it will not do any good. "She is an employee."

"Her mother was in a concentration camp," Bill says, as if that makes a difference.

"And pushed her way to the head of the line at the gas chamber?" I hear myself asking.

He is a solemn guy and not the kind of person with whom one risks that kind of joke.

He glares at me and turns away.

So that's how it is. I walk out to the parking lot and find my car. I sit down. But I can't drive away. Alice is inside.

My plan, then, which is not a plan, which makes no sense at all, is that I will just sit there, in the parking lot.

For ... three hours? Four?

For as long as it takes.

Or suppose I don't wait for her. Suppose I figure that it's all family and that someone will take her back to the hotel. That's not unreasonable. The other way to manage it would be to go back in there to let her know that I'm leaving.

No, I can't do that.

Can't go back, but I can't leave, either. Or, to put it more accurately, I could leave but I seem unable to summon up the will to put the key into the ignition and start the engine. I've been sitting here for some minutes and am unable to do anything. It is an interesting glimpse into the life of the catatonic. As George Orwell could have written, *Homage to Catatonia*. About all those Basque separatists unable to move or speak but resenting the hell out of how things are going in Spain.

Dan and Rainey have been of little help, I must say.

Maybe they, too, have been affected by this peculiar plague of silent immobility.

What to do?

> *Dan and Rainey are squatting by the campfire.*
> *From the darkness, an owl hoots.*

DAN: I don't know. (a short pause, and again) I don't know.

RAINEY: What don't you know?

DAN: I don't know.

RAINEY: You don't know?

DAN: I don't know.

RAINEY: (pause) What to do?

DAN: (immediately, as if in answer) I don't know.

RAINEY: You don't know?

DAN: I don't know.

RAINEY: You don't know what to do?

DAN: (after a pause, as if having considered this) What to do?

RAINEY: I don't know.

DAN: (finally) I don't know what to do.

RAINEY: Finally!

DAN: (after a pause) Finally?

RAINEY: Finally!

DAN: Finally, I don't know what to do.

RAINEY: You don't know what to do.

DAN: I don't know. What to do.

RAINEY: You don't know what to do? *I* don't know what to do.

DAN: What to do?

RAINEY: I don't know.

DAN: *I* don't know.

RAINEY: *We* don't know.

DAN: (after a pause) We don't *know*.

RAINEY: No idea.

DAN: (pause) No (pause) idea.

RAINEY: No idea what to do.

DAN: What to do?

RAINEY: No, no idea what to do.

DAN: *Yes*, "No idea what to do."

RAINEY: Yes. No idea.

DAN: What to do?

RAINEY: No idea what *to* do.

DAN: No idea *what* to do.

RAINEY: No idea what to *do*.

DAN: No *idea* what to do.

RAINEY: *No* idea what to do.

DAN: Well, that covers all the bases, doesn't it?

RAINEY: All the bases.

DAN: All the ducks in a row.

RAINEY: All the *ducks*?

DAN: All the ducks.

RAINEY: You think?

DAN: I think so. (A pause) But I don't know.

RAINEY: Back to that, are we?

DAN: Is there *anything* to do?

RAINEY: *Is* there anything to do?

DAN: Is there anything *to* do?

RAINEY: Is there anything to *do*?

DAN: (pause) Is *there* anything to do?

RAINEY: Well, that covers that, doesn't it?

DAN: All the ducks. On all the bases.

RAINEY: What sense does that make?

DAN: Sense? Who still believes in sense? More baggage it's good to be rid of.

RAINEY: More and more, you want less and less.

DAN: Soon you want nothing at all.

RAINEY: That's what we're looking for.

DAN: That's what we're looking to.

RAINEY: That's what we're looking *at*.

DAN: Staring it in the face.

RAINEY: Looking it right in the eye.

DAN: You can feel its hot breath.

RAINEY: You can?

DAN: In a manner of speaking.

RAINEY: Too vivid for me.

DAN: The eye is not too vivid, but the hot breath is?

RAINEY: Yeah.

DAN: I don't know…

It isn't the cavalry they've sent out to save me from the hostiles, but only my sister.

Or, actually, as I am about to discover, no one has sent her. She has come on her own, with a couple of glasses of champagne, which she holds in one hand while knocking with the other on the window to catch my attention.

"Alice."

I wonder why I have said her name. To prove that I remember it? To acknowledge her presence? To thank her?

No, it is more than that. It is a way of remarking on the absurd coincidence. It's a wedding, after all, and they're all in there, and we are out here, our parents' children, reunited again by our outsiderishness. And there is no way for me to allude gracefully to any of that except as I have already done, by the exclamation of her name.

"Well, open the door, for God's sake. Let me in."

"Oh, yes, sorry." I open the door. She hands me one of the flutes of champagne. I accept it, think for an instant about making a toast, realize that there is nothing I could possibly propose that wouldn't be sardonic and hurtful – to Malcolm, to Bill and Karyn, to Alice, or to myself. And I take a swallow.

"They send you out here to me?" I ask.

"No. But I noticed you weren't there."

I nod. We were seated next to each other and it wouldn't have been difficult for her to figure out that I'd disappeared.

"I expect Malcolm has noticed, too," she says.

"Yes. He's the only one I feel sorry about. Nina will have noticed, too, but she'll be delighted."

Alice nods in agreement.

"You going to come back?" she asks after a moment.

I shake my head slowly. "Can't."

"Why not?

I think about that for a bit. It isn't the photographer's push that I care about so much. It's … it's Bill, who should have fired her. Or at the least who should have apologized for her. There must have been something that he could have said that might have defused the situation.

But that nutty business about the woman's mother having been in a concentration camp, no matter how irrelevant, meant quite clearly that he was taking her side and rejecting my complaint. His judgment, his instincts, his sympathies were all with her. And my feelings were of no consequence.

I explain some of this to Alice, who is not unsympathetic.

And I have to turn away and pretend to be concentrating on the champagne, because I find it moving to be given even a glimpse of what it is supposed to feel like to have a sister. It isn't reliable. I'm not so stupid or crazy as to count on it, but I'd all but forgotten even how to imagine it.

"It's as if he'd broken the rules," she says, and she's quite right. Has the chemo caused wisdom as well as baldness? But that is it, exactly. I had a sense of what I was entitled to as the groom's father and as a guest, and he'd flouted all that, ignored it, and violated my most fundamental notions of how men and women are supposed to behave.

"He did," I agree. "I was his guest."

"But maybe he doesn't know those rules," Alice says.

"Are you defending him? Or making excuses?" I ask.

"No, no. Just trying to find a way for you to allow yourself to go back inside. For Malcolm's sake."

"I wish there were a way," I say, "but I don't see how."

Dad would have had a clear idea of the rules. And that's why he would have found it impossible to forgive the Kurtzes. And Alice. But, of course, I don't say any of that.

She is, if only for the moment, out here with me.

But as her death's-head face and the bizarre turban remind me, what the hell is there besides the moment? The time being?

The rest of it is a story.

But the idea of stories is inherently distorting. All those years of Dad's chagrin and rage and depression were not just a setup for this glimpse of payoff. That's what would happen in a novel, but novelists treat minor characters with a ruthlessness that would make God blush.

For Alice to be sitting here in the car with me for five minutes doesn't make up for his suffering.

But then, nothing can.

For her to be here does speak to it, though. In my mind, anyway.

And I have the eerie idea that, in her turban and her gauntness, she is closer to Dad now than I am. It is not the rapprochement either of them might have expected.

To change the subject for myself to something less grisly, I think of Ronnie, who only a few months ago sat where she is sitting, with an altogether different set of troubles and a demonstration of other shortcomings in the condition of brother- and sister-hood.

I can't tell Alice about either of these odd observations.

"Well," Alice says, reverting to the immediate practical questions that face us, "if you can't go back in there, shall I go in and say goodbye for you? To Malcolm?"

I nod.

"You don't mind that he's staying," she says, a question, but spoken without that interrogative upturn at the end.

"No. It's his wedding."

She nods.

"And what about Jason?" she asks.

"Tell him, too."

"You don't mind if he stays?"

"I'd rather he did. They should be together. What happened to me doesn't require any response from them."

"You want more wine?" she offers.

I shake my head, no. I have to drive. And it's Bill and Karyn's wine, after all.

"I'll be back," Alice says. "You'll wait for me."

"You don't have to leave the party," I tell her.

"Yes, I do."

7

So what do I suppose she is thinking? Is she making the same kinds of connections and thinking about the same disasters? Is her behavior here with me any kind of conscious attempt to make up for her mistakes and misdeeds of the past?

I hope not. Because that would be painful for her.

And having benefited from these small kindnesses of hers, I am reluctant to have her undergo any further discomfort.

I can't guess how much she is able, for her own benefit and mine, to deny.

I can't guess what Malcolm is thinking, either, but I am not much worried. He is thinking about Joanne. If he is thinking of me, he is being generous, realizing that a) I am a lunatic, and b) if I have disappeared, it is in order to spare him and myself and even Bill and Karyn further unpleasantness.

And Jason is there, so he's not alone.

Nina is there, too, of course. She is exultant. She couldn't possibly be having a better time than to think of me skulking away like this, fleeing from the party like Cinderella in a pumpkin drawn by rats.

Or was it the coachman who was a rat?

Who cares? The point is that I can expect from Malcolm some generosity, some allowance, that one is able to assume when, underneath everything else, there is love.

And realizing that is enough to make me pleased. Not happy, maybe, which is beyond my repertoire, but there's a source of pleasure. And pride.

Even if he's displeased with me, I am confident that he will forgive me. And that's saying a lot, too.

❖

The only trouble with Alice's otherwise reasonable plan is that it leaves me alone here in the car while she goes back to let Malcolm know that I am leaving and offer whatever excuses or insults she can think of to Bill and Karyn.

And on my own, I am vulnerable to bad thoughts.

As for instance the idea that this has to have been planned. There is a design here. It's too intricate for real life, too well shaped. There were fifteen people that Belsen alumna's daughter could have chosen to assault, but there I was.

Was it only Murphy's Law, that whatever can go wrong will?

Or was some divinity working this out? Is this the fulfillment of a scheme that has been in the works for twenty years and more? Some novelist jots notes on a yellow pad, and, a hundred pages later, a woman pushes some guy at a wedding.

Well, that can happen, sure. But if the novelist is God? Then we have, perhaps, messieurs-dames, an explanation of the difficulties in Rwanda and Bosnia. All the catastrophes of the twentieth century may be explained by the curious and horrific thought that God has found himself a hobby. This universe isn't interesting enough for him. So he meddles. He has, perhaps, been reading E. M. Forster, and he is possessed by the idea that this is how his creation should be organized.

And there are, here and there, populations, countries, continents to which he is paying insufficient attention. None at all, actually.

They're such minor characters, they don't even appear!

In any humane attempt to describe the texture and quality of modern life, there ought to be at least an indication that, outside the frame of our attention, there are tornadoes and massacres, that most of Africa is dying of AIDS, that horrors are happening that may not be important to us but ought, nonetheless, to be mentioned.

The Nepalese royal family gets blown away by the Crown Prince who is declared King and is then taken off the ventilator, or perhaps smothered with a pillow by the Maoist head of the Security Service? And it has nothing to do with this novel, which is why it happened. God hasn't been paying attention. He has been occupied in making sure that Ilsa gets this wedding to shoot.

(Ilsa? Her mother was an admirer of Frau Koch? Or grateful at not having been turned into a lampshade? Why not? It's as plausible as anything else, isn't it? Which was what Forster was too refined to acknowledge.)

So I frame my little prayer to God. Just leave me alone. Give up this idea of becoming a novelist. You are the Lord, King of Heaven and Earth, and you do not need to be nominated for the Faulkner Prize. Or the Pulitzer or the Nobel. You do not want to be booked on Imus or taken to lunch by some editor from Alfred A. Knopf. Put this in a drawer, the way most sensible, grown-up people do eventually, and get on with the business of life in the world. Save the tigers. Save the Bosñeros. And leave me alone, would you, please? Amen.

❖

Where is she? What is she doing and saying? What is she thinking?

I haven't the vaguest idea. Which is another problem with novels. We suppose what other people are thinking, but we know that our suppositions are at best approximate. I am not even sure, at any given moment, what I'm thinking.

Nobody can be. Which was why Freud distrusted biography and believed that the psychotherapeutic encounter had to be vis-à-vis and oral. Written words are already falsified – that is to say, edited – by the time the ink has dried on the paper. In the space between the words a diffident thought presents itself, only to be dismissed, because the writer isn't brave enough to pursue it. He (or she) settles for what is conventionally correct. Reasonable. Decorous. Expected.

Civilized.

As if there were any such thing.

Civilization and Its Discotheques.

There were mornings when Ahab looked out at the sun-dappled sea and felt great. Not a care in the world. Nothing but a school of dancing porpoises. But they were irrelevant to Melville's schooled purposes. And even though they were there, and appeared, they do not appear.

Alice seems not to be appearing, either.

I can send out a party for her. Winnetou would be right at home here. More horseshit to pick up and sniff than any red-blooded and red-skinned injun could shake a feathered stick at.

I could go, myself.

No, I couldn't. I'll just stay here and think. Wondering whether Alice hasn't planned all this in order to set me up, to raise my expectations that she will, in some dramatic way, dash.

An ungenerous thought.

But, in our gens, not an unprecedented one.

In any event, it's incorrect. There she is.

She opens the car door and gets in.

"It's okay," she says. "We can go now. It's all right. Malcolm's sorry but he said he understands."

"Thanks."

Of course, it isn't all right. It's all wrong. Or, worse, they're wrong. If I were wrong, I could apologize, back down, and beg to be forgiven. But the certainty that I'm right is a terrible burden. This is what froze my father into that paralysis of grief of his last years, his belief that he had behaved correctly and that they hadn't, the Kurtzes and Alice. And that left him nowhere to go, nothing to do, no escape other than to abandon what he believed about what men and women owe each other in the way of ethical behavior and justice.

I can't say any of this to Alice. There is only the silence that hangs between us, as if it were the smell from one of those pine-tree-shaped car deodorizers that people mount on their rearview mirrors. Are these people smokers? Do they fart a lot? What is the marketing strategy to reach them? I'd prefer the smell of farts — of my own, surely. Auden says somewhere that we all love the look of our own handwriting, the way we like the smell of our own farts. He was being naughty and aggressively faggy, daring us to love him anyway, but he won because we did.

But the point is — and there is one, actually — that, like some farts, this silence is not all that unpleasant. She is here with me, my sister, and we have fled, if that's the verb I am going to settle for, together. We are right and here, and they are wrong and there.

And we are not saying anything because we don't have to.

Or not for a while, anyway. There are practical questions to be decided.

The timing of my confrontation was such that Alice and I missed the meal. Didn't even have the hors d'oeuvres. None of that expensive spread. Which is fine with me, but I am a little hungry. As Alice may be, too.

"You want to stop for a bite?" I ask.

"If you're up to it, sure."

"I'm up to it."

I have a recollection of a paragraph in ... Dale Carnegie? One of those old self-helpers, anyway. It was about going to somebody's expensive house where there was bickering and yelling and arguing, and the wife dropped the roast beef on the floor, and Carnegie, or whoever it was, tells us that he'd rather have a hot dog from a cart on the corner in peace and quiet than roast beef in a well-appointed house with silver and crystal and fine china on the table and all this bickering.

And what sticks in my mind is the hot dog.

Do I suggest that we drive – two hundred miles? – to the Log Cabin? Of course not. More likely than not, it isn't there anymore, anyway.

But a hot dog would be nice.

Maybe a diner, then? I suggest that. And Alice of course agrees. Whatever I want.

We find one, not absolutely authentic, not a classic diner like, say, the Blue Ben up in Bennington, but one of those extravagant New Jersey versions. A diner that has suffered the curse of abundance and prosperity. And I pull off and park in its elaborately landscaped parking area, and we go inside and take a booth. Alice orders an egg-white omelet with mushrooms and green peppers. And I order the hot dog special.

The waitress pours us coffee, decaf for Alice and regular for me, and after a very short wait she comes back with the food. Alice looks at my hot dogs and asks for a bite. Which is odd for her.

But, sure, I cut her off a piece of one of them, and she spears it with her fork and dips it in my mustard.

"Remember the Log Cabin?" she asks.

"That's exactly what I was thinking about," I tell her. "That's why I ordered this."

She nods. She rubs her eyes a little.

Nobody says anything. Nobody has to.

8

*If it was not for death and marriage I do not know
how the average novelist would conclude. Death and
marriage are almost his only connection between his
characters and his plot, and the reader is more ready
to meet him here, and take a bookish view of them,
provided they occur later on in the book: the writer,
poor fellow, must be allowed to finish up somehow, he
has his living to get like anyone else, so no wonder
that nothing is heard but hammering and screwing.*

—E. M. Forster, *Aspects of the Novel*

The sounds of screwing? Surely he didn't mean it that way.
But what other way is there?

Come on, Eddie, pay attention, will you?

But it is not my purpose here to twit him. It's an
interesting and useful book, and it teaches us a great deal.
It's more interesting, perhaps, to readers of novels than to
writers, but there are more readers than writers. (In fiction,
anyway, that's true. In poetry? Go know.)

But what I'm working up to here is an ending, as
you've already noticed, having realized that the sheaf of
pages on the right-hand side is much thinner than it used
to be, and almost the whole book is now on the left.

It's an interesting mimesis of mortality, isn't it? These
characters, although notional and immortal, seem to exist
in time, and the time left to them seems to be dwindling.

But how do we get out of this? A death? A marriage?
We've been there. We've been there the whole time.

And to have a climax in which a character gives a piece
of his frankfurter to his sister is so silly as to defy any possibility of a graceful and appropriately elegiac dénouement.

Beats the hell out of me, I freely admit.

But God is more ambitious. He is perhaps angling to get himself elected to the Fellowship of Southern Writers or the American Academy of Arts and Letters, and he wants to show off with some desperate, brilliant save.

So what does he do?

A month later, I find a small box in my mailbox. It's brown cardboard, four inches by four inches and four-and-a-half inches high. My name and address are printed in block letters. No return address. Ninety-seven cents' worth of stamps.

I am not expecting anything like it. And I am puzzled because of the anonymity. From whom, from where? I am not frightened, but I shake it a little, and feel its heft.

It's not a bomb. It's not heavy enough to be dangerous. (That's what I think!)

So I take it inside and open it up.

A baggie filled with … ashes.

And a letter, an old letter of mine addressed to Nina. From forty years ago, when we were just beginning our courtship.

The penny drops. The ashes are all the letters but this one, which has been spared only to show what the ashes came from. And even this seems to have been an after-thought, because the upper right-hand corner of the envelope has been singed. This was snatched from the fire. It is a second, crueler, and more refined thought.

Figure that she was doing some serious cleaning and that this box turned up with the letters in it. And figure, too, that she'd seen me implode at the wedding, had heard about my encounter with the aggressive photographer, and had concluded that I was there, on the edge, waiting to be pushed over. Might not this be enough to do the trick?

And even if it failed, it was a nice display of contempt.

Not the letters but only their ashes, after all.

How to reply?

Not to her. There was nothing to say to her. But to the gesture. What gesture could I make in return? What dénouement could I contrive that would be satisfactory to myself, would be artistically pleasing?

I read the single surviving letter, my own letter of many years before, recognize my old stationery, my crabbed handwriting. I also recognize the banter and can recall, just barely, the lust that prompted some of it. And the love?

No, I can't remember that. That seems now ... erroneous. Delusional. I can't imagine what that young man could have been thinking.

But he's me, obviously. And these are his ashes.

The decent thing to do with them is ... what's usual and customary with ashes.

I put on a windbreaker and stick the baggie in my pocket. I go for a walk. And in ten minutes I am on a bridge over the river. There's a slight wind, enough to whip the surface of the river into little wavelets. And on the downwind side of the bridge I take out the baggie and open it, letting the wind take the ashes and scatter them.

A brief flurry of ashes that dissipates and floats down to the surface of the water.

Old words.

It's a quirky thing to be doing. Or to have done, because it's already floating out to sea and into the past. What did I mean by it, exactly?

Forgiven? Forgotten? Or just moving on, which may be almost as good?

I don't know.

I stand there for a few minutes, not even trying to sort it out, but just looking at the water. Then I look up at a sky with clouds scudding high overhead. There isn't any God there. Or none that I can see. Maybe he is already occupied elsewhere, figuring out some elegant conclusion for some other poor son of a bitch.

As far as he's concerned, I am all but forgotten, a passing figment, like those words on the letters, or like these. Like Steve and Leo, and Timmy and Donna, and Dan and Rainey, all of whom, I realize, have left me alone for some weeks now.

Thanks, Beater God, as some kids say, not knowing better, or maybe knowing better than their parents.

Yet another instance of tmesis? No, no. The opposite, actually. That would be a crasis.

David R. Slavitt is the author of sixteen novels and, in all, seventy works of fiction, poetry, and poetry and drama in translation. His most recent books are the poetry collection *Falling from Silence*, the pair of novellas *Get Thee to a Nunnery: A Pair of Shakespearean Divertimentos*, and the poetry translation (from Latin) *Propertius in Love: The Complete Poetry*. He teaches literature and writing at Bennington College and lives in Cambridge, Massachusetts.

This book was set in the Adobe Berling Roman typeface. The text and the jacket were printed by Phoenix Color Corp. in Hagerstown, Maryland. Both book and jacket were designed by Robert Wechsler.

Catbird Press specializes in American and British literature, Czech literature in translation, and sophisticated humor. For more information about Catbird, please visit our website, www. catbirdpress.com, or request a catalog from catalog@catbirdpress. com, 800-360-2391, or Catbird Press, 16 Windsor Road, North Haven, CT 06473-3015.